Ghosts I Have Met and Some Others

by

John Kendrick Bangs

Ghosts I Have Met and Some Others
by John Kendrick Bangs

Copyright © 2023

All Rights reserved.
No part of this publication may be reproduced, stored in a retrieval system, or transmitted in any form or by any means, electronic, mechanical, photocopying or Otherwise, without the written permission of the publisher.

The author/editor asserts the moral right to be identified as the author/editor of this work.

ISBN: 978-93-57486-55-2

Published by

DOUBLE 9 BOOKS

2/13-B, Ansari Road
Daryaganj, New Delhi – 110002
info@double9books.com
www.double9books.com
Tel. 011-40042856

This book is under public domain

ABOUT THE AUTHOR

John Kendrick Bangs was an American writer, humorist, editor, and satirist who lived from May 27, 1862, to January 21, 1922. Yonkers, New York, is where he was born. Francis S. Bangs and his brother Francis N. Bangs worked as a lawyer in New York City. Bangs earned a Bachelor of Philosophy in Political Science from Columbia College in 1883. He edited the literary journal Acta Columbia at Columbia and wrote brief, anonymous pieces for humor magazines. Bangs also briefly held the position of Munsey's Magazine's first editor. Bangs unsuccessfully ran for mayor of Yonkers, New York, in 1894. He delivered a speech in 1918 to YMCA members and allied soldiers on the front lines in France. He was well-known in the "Profile Cottage" circles as a jokester and prankster in addition to being a sarcastic author. In 1901, he departed Harper & Brothers, and in 1903, he was appointed editor of the New Metropolitan publication. He was named editor of Puck in 1904, which was maybe the best American humor publication at the time. He shifted his attention to the lecture circuit in 1906. At the age of 59, he passed away from stomach cancer in Atlantic City, New Jersey.

CONTENTS

GHOSTS THAT HAVE HAUNTED ME 7

THE MYSTERY OF MY GRANDMOTHER'S
HAIR SOFA 19

THE MYSTERY OF BARNEY O'ROURKE 27

THE EXORCISM THAT FAILED 34

THURLOW'S CHRISTMAS STORY 58

THE DAMPMERE MYSTERY 72

CARLETON BARKER, FIRST AND SECOND 78

GHOSTS THAT HAVE HAUNTED ME

A FEW SPIRIT REMINISCENCES

If we could only get used to the idea that ghosts are perfectly harmless creatures, who are powerless to affect our well-being unless we assist them by giving way to our fears, we should enjoy the supernatural exceedingly, it seems to me. Coleridge, I think it was, was once asked by a lady if he believed in ghosts, and he replied, "No, madame; I have seen too many of them." Which is my case exactly. I have seen so many horrid visitants from other worlds that they hardly affect me at all, so far as the mere inspiration of terror is concerned. On the other hand, they interest me hugely; and while I must admit that I do experience all the purely physical sensations that come from horrific encounters of this nature, I can truly add in my own behalf that mentally I can rise above the physical impulse to run away, and, invariably standing my ground, I have gained much useful information concerning them. I am prepared to assert that if a thing with flashing green eyes, and clammy hands, and long, dripping strips of sea-weed in place of hair, should rise up out of the floor before me at this moment, 2 A.M., and nobody in the house but myself, with a fearful, nerve-destroying storm raging outside, I should without hesitation ask it to sit down and light a cigar and state its business—or, if it were of the female persuasion, to join me in a bottle of sarsaparilla—although every physical manifestation of fear of which my poor body is capable would be present. I have had experiences in this line which, if I could get you to believe them, would convince you that I speak the truth. Knowing weak, suspicious human nature as I do, however, I do not hope ever to convince you—though it is none the less true— that on one occasion, in the spring of 1895, there was a spiritual manifestation in my library which nearly prostrated me physically, but which mentally I hugely enjoyed, because I was mentally strong enough to subdue my physical repugnance for the thing which suddenly and without any apparent reason materialized in my arm-chair.

I'm going to tell you about it briefly, though I warn you in advance that you will find it a great strain upon your confidence in my veracity. It may even shatter that confidence beyond repair; but I cannot help that. I hold that it is a man's duty in this life to give to the world the benefit of his experience. All that he sees he should set down exactly as he sees it, and so simply, withal, that to the dullest comprehension the moral involved shall be perfectly obvious. If he is a painter, and an auburn-haired maiden appears to him to have blue hair, he should paint her hair blue, and just so long as he sticks by his principles and is true to himself, he need not bother about what you may think of him. So it is with me. My scheme of living is based upon being true to myself. You may class me with Baron Munchausen if you choose; I shall not mind so long as I have the consolation of feeling, deep down in my heart, that I am a true realist, and diverge not from the paths of truth as truth manifests itself to me.

This intruder of whom I was just speaking, the one that took possession of my arm-chair in the spring of 1895, was about as horrible a spectre as I have ever had the pleasure to have haunt me. It was worse than grotesque. It grated on every nerve. Alongside of it the ordinary poster of the present day would seem to be as accurate in drawing as a bicycle map, and in its coloring it simply shrieked with discord.

If color had tones which struck the ear, instead of appealing to the eye, the thing would have deafened me. It was about midnight when the manifestation first took shape. My family had long before retired, and I had just finished smoking a cigar—which was one of a thousand which my wife had bought for me at a Monday sale at one of the big department stores in New York. I don't remember the brand, but that is just as well—it was not a cigar to be advertised in a civilized piece of literature—but I do remember that they came in bundles of fifty, tied about with blue ribbon. The one I had been smoking tasted and burned as if it had been rolled by a Cuban insurrectionist while fleeing from a Spanish regiment through a morass, gathering its component parts as he ran. It had two distinct merits, however. No man could possibly smoke too many of them, and they were economical, which is how the ever-helpful little madame came to get them for me, and

I have no doubt they will some day prove very useful in removing insects from the rose-bushes. They cost $3.99 a thousand on five days a week, but at the Monday sale they were marked down to $1.75, which is why my wife, to whom I had recently read a little lecture on economy, purchased them for me. Upon the evening in question I had been at work on this cigar for about two hours, and had smoked one side of it three-quarters of the way down to the end, when I concluded that I had smoked enough—for one day—so I rose up to cast the other side into the fire, which was flickering fitfully in my spacious fireplace. This done, I turned about, and there, fearful to see, sat this thing grinning at me from the depths of my chair. My hair not only stood on end, but tugged madly in an effort to get away. Four hairs—I can prove the statement if it be desired—did pull themselves loose from my scalp in their insane desire to rise above the terrors of the situation, and, flying upward, stuck like nails into the oak ceiling directly over my head, whence they had to be pulled the next morning with nippers by our hired man, who would no doubt testify to the truth of the occurrence as I have asserted it if he were still living, which, unfortunately, he is not. Like most hired men, he was subject to attacks of lethargy, from one of which he died last summer. He sank into a rest about weed-time, last June, and lingered quietly along for two months, and after several futile efforts to wake him up, we finally disposed of him to our town crematory for experimental purposes. I am told he burned very actively, and I believe it, for to my certain knowledge he was very dry, and not so green as some persons who had previously employed him affected to think. A cold chill came over me as my eye rested upon the horrid visitor and noted the greenish depths of his eyes and the claw-like formation of his fingers, and my flesh began to creep like an inch-worm. At one time I was conscious of eight separate corrugations on my back, and my arms goose-fleshed until they looked like one of those miniature plaster casts of the Alps which are so popular in Swiss summer resorts; but mentally I was not disturbed at all. My repugnance was entirely physical, and, to come to the point at once, I calmly offered the spectre a cigar, which it accepted, and demanded a light. I gave it, nonchalantly lighting the match upon the goose-fleshing of my wrist.

Now I admit that this was extraordinary and hardly credible, yet it happened exactly as I have set it down, and, furthermore, I enjoyed the experience. For three hours the thing and I conversed, and not once during that time did my hair stop pulling away at my scalp, or the repugnance cease to run in great rolling waves up and down my back. If I wished to deceive you, I might add that pin-feathers began to grow from the goose-flesh, but that would be a lie, and lying and I are not friends, and, furthermore, this paper is not written to amaze, but to instruct.

Except for its personal appearance, this particular ghost was not very remarkable, and I do not at this time recall any of the details of our conversation beyond the point that my share of it was not particularly coherent, because of the discomfort attendant upon the fearful hair-pulling process I was going through. I merely cite its coming to prove that, with all the outward visible signs of fear manifesting themselves in no uncertain manner, mentally I was cool enough to cope with the visitant, and sufficiently calm and at ease to light the match upon my wrist, perceiving for the first time, with an Edison-like ingenuity, one of the uses to which goose-flesh might be put, and knowing full well that if I tried to light it on the sole of my shoe I should have fallen to the ground, my knees being too shaky to admit of my standing on one leg even for an instant. Had I been mentally overcome, I should have tried to light the match on my foot, and fallen ignominiously to the floor then and there.

There was another ghost that I recall to prove my point, who was of very great use to me in the summer immediately following the spring of which I have just told you. You will possibly remember how that the summer of 1895 had rather more than its fair share of heat, and that the lovely New Jersey town in which I have the happiness to dwell appeared to be the headquarters of the temperature. The thermometers of the nation really seemed to take orders from Beachdale, and properly enough, for our town is a born leader in respect to heat. Having no property to sell, I candidly admit that Beachdale is not of an arctic nature in summer, except socially, perhaps. Socially, it is the coolest town in the State; but we are at this moment not discussing cordiality, fraternal love, or the question raised by the Declaration of Independence as to whether all men are born equal. The warmth we have in hand is what the old lady called "Fahrenheat," and, from a thermometric point of view, Beachdale, if I may be a trifle slangy, as I sometimes am, has heat to burn. There are mitigations of this heat, it is true, but they generally come along in winter.

I must claim, in behalf of my town, that never in all my experience have I known a summer so hot that it was not, sooner or later—by January, anyhow—followed by a cool spell. But in the summer of 1895 even the real-estate agents confessed that the cold wave announced by the weather bureau at Washington summered elsewhere—in the tropics, perhaps, but not at Beachdale. One hardly dared take a bath in the morning for fear of being scalded by the fluid that flowed from the cold-water faucet—our reservoir is entirely unprotected by shade-trees, and in summer a favorite spot for young Waltons who like to catch bass already boiled—my neighbors and myself lived on cracked ice, ice-cream, and destructive cold drinks. I do not myself mind hot weather in the daytime, but hot nights are killing. I can't sleep. I toss about for hours, and then, for the sake of variety, I flop, but sleep cometh not. My debts double, and my income seems to sizzle away under the influence of a hot, sleepless night; and it was just here that a certain awful thing saved me from the insanity which is a certain result of parboiled insomnia.

It was about the 16th of July, which, as I remember reading in an extra edition of the *Evening Bun*, got out to mention the fact, was the hottest 16th of July known in thirty-eight years. I had retired at half-past seven, after dining lightly upon a cold salmon and a gallon of iced tea—not because I was tired, but because I wanted to get down to first principles at once, and remove my clothing, and sort of spread myself over all the territory I could, which is a thing you can't do in a library, or even in a white-and-gold parlor. If man were constructed like a machine, as he really ought to be, to be strictly comfortable—a machine that could be taken apart like an eight-day clock—I should have taken myself apart, putting one section of myself on the roof, another part in the spare room, hanging a third on the clothes-line in the yard, and so on, leaving my head in the ice-box; but unfortunately we have to keep ourselves together in this life, hence I did the only thing one can do, and retired, and incidentally spread myself over some freshly baked bedclothing. There was some relief from the heat, but not much. I had been roasting, and while my sensations were somewhat like those which I imagine come to a planked shad when he first finds himself spread out over the plank, there was a mitigation. My temperature fell off from 167 to about 163, which is not quite enough to make a man absolutely content. Suddenly, however, I began to shiver. There was no breeze, but I began to shiver.

"It is getting cooler," I thought, as the chill came on, and I rose and looked at the thermometer. It still registered the highest possible point, and the mercury was rebelliously trying to break through the top of the glass tube and take a stroll on the roof.

"That's queer," I said to myself. "It's as hot as ever, and yet I'm shivering. I wonder if my goose is cooked? I've certainly got a chill."

I jumped back into bed and pulled the sheet up over me; but still I shivered. Then I pulled the blanket up, but the chill continued. I couldn't seem to get warm again. Then came the counterpane, and finally I had to put on my bath-robe—a fuzzy woollen affair, which in midwinter I had sometimes found too warm for comfort. Even then I was not sufficiently bundled up, so I called for an extra blanket, two afghans, and the hot-water bag.

Everybody in the house thought I had gone mad, and I wondered myself if perhaps I hadn't, when all of a sudden I perceived, off in the corner, the Awful Thing, and perceiving it, I knew all.

I was being haunted, and the physical repugnance of which I have spoken was on. The cold shiver, the invariable accompaniment of the ghostly visitant, had come, and I assure you I never was so glad of anything in my life. It has always been said of me by my critics that I am raw; I was afraid that after that night they would say I was half baked, and I would far rather be the one than the other; and it was the Awful Thing that saved me. Realizing this, I spoke to it gratefully.

"You are a heaven-born gift on a night like this," said I, rising up and walking to its side.

"I am glad to be of service to you," the Awful Thing replied, smiling at me so yellowly that I almost wished the author of the *Blue-Button of Cowardice* could have seen it.

"It's very good of you," I put in.

"Not at all," replied the Thing; "you are the only man I know who doesn't think it necessary to prevaricate about ghosts every time he gets an order for a Christmas story. There have been more lies told about us than about any other class of things in existence, and we are getting a trifle tired of it. We may have lost our corporeal existence, but some of our sensitiveness still remains."

"Well," said I, rising and lighting the gas-logs—for I was on the very verge of congealment—"I am sure I am pleased if you like my stories."

"Oh, as for that, I don't think much of them," said the Awful Thing, with a purple display of candor which amused me, although I cannot say that I relished it; "but you never lie about us. You are not at all interesting, but you are truthful, and we spooks hate libellers. Just because one happens to be a thing is no reason why writers should libel it, and that's why I have always respected you. We regard you as a sort of spook Boswell. You may be dull and stupid, but you tell the truth, and when I saw you in imminent danger of becoming a mere grease spot, owing to the fearful heat, I decided to help you through. That's why I'm here. Go to sleep now. I'll stay here and keep you shivering until daylight anyhow. I'd stay longer, but we are always laid at sunrise."

"Like an egg," I said, sleepily.

"Tutt!" said the ghost. "Go to sleep, If you talk I'll have to go."

And so I dropped off to sleep as softly and as sweetly as a tired child. In the morning I awoke refreshed. The rest of my family were prostrated, but I was fresh. The Awful Thing was gone, and the room was warming up again; and if it had not been for the tinkling ice in my water-pitcher, I should have suspected it was all a dream. And so throughout the whole sizzling summer the friendly spectre stood by me and kept me cool, and I haven't a doubt that it was because of his good offices in keeping me shivering on those fearful August nights that I survived the season, and came to my work in the autumn as fit as a fiddle—so fit, indeed, that I have not written a poem since that has not struck me as being the very best of its kind, and if I can find a publisher who will take the risk of putting those poems out, I shall unequivocally and without hesitation acknowledge, as I do here, my debt of gratitude to my friends in the spirit world.

Manifestations of this nature, then, are harmful, as I have already observed, only when the person who is haunted yields to his physical impulses. Fought stubbornly inch by inch with the will, they can be subdued, and often they are a boon. I think I have proved both these points. It took me a long time to discover the facts, however, and my discovery came about in this way. It may perhaps interest you to know how I made it. I encountered at the English home of a wealthy friend at one time a "presence" of an insulting turn of mind. It was at my friend Jarley's little baronial hall, which he had rented from the Earl of Brokedale the year Mrs. Jarley was presented at court. The Countess of Brokedale's social influence went with the château for a slightly increased rental, which was why the Jarleys took it. I was invited to spend a month with them, not so much because Jarley is fond of me as because Mrs. Jarley had a sort of an idea that, as a writer, I might say something about their newly acquired glory in some American Sunday newspaper; and Jarley laughingly assigned to me the "haunted chamber," without at least one of which no baronial hall in the old country is considered worthy of the name.

"It will interest you more than any other," Jarley said; "and if it has a ghost, I imagine you will be able to subdue him."

I gladly accepted the hospitality of my friend, and was delighted at his consideration in giving me the haunted chamber, where I might pursue my investigations into the subject of phantoms undisturbed. Deserting London, then, for a time, I ran down to Brokedale Hall, and took up my abode there with a half-dozen other guests. Jarley, as usual since his sudden "gold-fall," as Wilkins called it, did everything with a lavish hand. I believe a man could have got diamonds on toast if he had chosen to ask for them. However, this is apart from my story.

I had occupied the haunted chamber about two weeks before anything of importance occurred, and then it came—and a more unpleasant, ill-mannered spook never floated in the ether. He materialized about 3 A.M. and was unpleasantly sulphurous to one's perceptions. He sat upon the divan in my room, holding his knees in his hands, leering and scowling upon me as though I were the intruder, and not he.

"Who are you?" I asked, excitedly, as in the dying light of the log fire he loomed grimly up before me.

"None of your business," he replied, insolently, showing his teeth as he spoke. "On the other hand, who are you? This is my room, and not yours, and it is I who have the right to question. If you have any business here, well and good. If not, you will oblige me by removing yourself, for your presence is offensive to me."

"I am a guest in the house," I answered, restraining my impulse to throw the inkstand at him for his impudence. "And this room has been set apart for my use by my host."

"One of the servant's guests, I presume?" he said, insultingly, his lividly lavender-like lip upcurling into a haughty sneer, which was maddening to a self-respecting worm like myself.

I rose up from my bed, and picked up the poker to bat him over the head, but again I restrained myself. It will not do to quarrel, I thought. I will be courteous if he is not, thus giving a dead Englishman a lesson which wouldn't hurt some of the living.

"No," I said, my voice tremulous with wrath—"no; I am the guest of my friend Mr. Jarley, an American, who—"

"Same thing," observed the intruder, with a yellow sneer. "Race of low-class animals, those Americans—only fit for gentlemen's stables, you know."

This was too much. A ghost may insult me with impunity, but when he tackles my people he must look out for himself. I sprang forward with an ejaculation of wrath, and with all my strength struck at him with the poker, which I still held in my hand. If he had been anything but a ghost, he would have been split vertically from top to toe; but as it was, the poker passed harmlessly through his misty make-up, and rent a great gash two feet long in Jarley's divan. The yellow sneer faded from his lips, and a maddening blue smile took its place.

"Humph!" he observed, nonchalantly. "What a useless ebullition, and what a vulgar display of temper! Really you are the most humorous insect I have yet encountered. From what part of the States do you come? I am truly interested to know in what kind of soil exotics of your peculiar kind are cultivated. Are you part of the fauna or the flora of your tropical States—or what?"

And then I realized the truth. There is no physical method of combating a ghost which can result in his discomfiture, so I resolved to try the intellectual. It was a mind-to-mind contest, and he was easy prey after I got going. I joined him in his blue smile, and began to talk about the English aristocracy; for I doubted not, from the spectre's manner, that he was or had been one of that class. He had about him that haughty lack of manners which bespoke the aristocrat. I waxed very eloquent when, as I say, I got my mind really going. I spoke of kings and queens and their uses in no uncertain phrases, of divine right, of dukes, earls, marquises—of all the pompous establishments of British royalty and nobility—with that contemptuously humorous tolerance of a necessary and somewhat amusing evil which we find in American comic papers. We had a battle royal for about one hour, and I must confess he was a foeman worthy of any man's steel, so long as I was reasonable in my arguments; but when I finally observed that it wouldn't be ten years before Barnum and Bailey's Greatest Show on Earth had the whole lot engaged for the New York circus season, stalking about the Madison Square Garden arena, with the Prince of Wales at the head beating a tomtom, he grew iridescent with wrath, and fled madly through the wainscoting of the room. It was purely a mental victory. All the physical possibilities of my being would have exhausted themselves futilely before him; but when I turned upon him the resources of my fancy, my imagination unrestrained, and held back by no sense of responsibility, he was as a child in my hands, obstreperous but certain to be subdued. If it were not for Mrs. Jarley's wrath—which, I admit, she tried to conceal—over the damage to her divan, I should now look back upon that visitation as the most agreeable haunting experience of my life; at any rate, it was at that time that I first learned how to handle ghosts, and since that time I have been able to overcome them without trouble— save in one instance, with which I shall close this chapter of my reminiscences, and which I give only to prove the necessity of observing strictly one point in dealing with spectres.

It happened last Christmas, in my own home. I had provided as a little surprise for my wife a complete new solid silver service marked with her initials. The tree had been prepared for the children, and all had retired save myself. I had lingered later than the others to put the silver service under the tree, where its happy recipient would find it when she went to the tree with the little ones the next morning. It made a magnificent display: the two dozen of each kind of spoon, the forks, the knives, the coffee-pot, water-urn, and all; the salvers, the vegetable-dishes, olive-forks, cheese-scoops, and other dazzling attributes of a complete service, not to go into details, presented a fairly scintillating picture which would have made me gasp if I had not, at the moment when my own breath began to catch, heard another gasp in the corner immediately behind me. Turning about quickly to see whence it came, I observed a dark figure in the pale light of the moon which streamed in through the window.

"Who are you?" I cried, starting back, the physical symptoms of a ghostly presence manifesting themselves as usual.

"I am the ghost of one long gone before," was the reply, in sepulchral tones.

I breathed a sigh of relief, for I had for a moment feared it was a burglar.

"Oh!" I said. "You gave me a start at first. I was afraid you were a material thing come to rob me." Then turning towards the tree, I observed, with a wave of the hand, "Fine lay out, eh?"

"Beautiful," he said, hollowly. "Yet not so beautiful as things I've seen in realms beyond your ken."

And then he set about telling me of the beautiful gold and silver ware they used in the Elysian Fields, and I must confess Monte Cristo would have had a hard time, with Sindbad the Sailor to help, to surpass the picture of royal magnificence the spectre drew. I stood inthralled until, even as he was talking, the clock struck three, when he rose up, and moving slowly across the floor, barely visible, murmured regretfully that he must be off, with which he faded away down the back stairs. I pulled my nerves, which were getting rather strained, together again, and went to bed.

Next morning every bit of that silver-ware was gone; and, what is more, three weeks later I found the ghost's picture in the Rogues' Gallery in New York as that of the cleverest sneak-thief in the country.

All of which, let me say to you, dear reader, in conclusion, proves that when you are dealing with ghosts you mustn't give up all your physical resources until you have definitely ascertained that the thing by which you are confronted, horrid or otherwise, is a ghost, and not an all too material rogue with a light step, and a commodious jute bag for plunder concealed beneath his coat.

"How to tell a ghost?" you ask.

Well, as an eminent master of fiction frequently observes in his writings, "that is another story," which I shall hope some day to tell for your instruction and my own aggrandizement.

THE MYSTERY OF MY GRANDMOTHER'S HAIR SOFA

It happened last Christmas Eve, and precisely as I am about to set it forth. It has been said by critics that I am a romancer of the wildest sort, but that is where my critics are wrong. I grant that the experiences through which I have passed, some of which have contributed to the gray matter in my hair, however little they may have augmented that within my cranium—experiences which I have from time to time set forth to the best of my poor abilities in the columns of such periodicals as I have at my mercy—have been of an order so excessively supernatural as to give my critics a basis for their aspersions; but they do not know, as I do, that that basis is as uncertain as the shifting sands of the sea, inasmuch as in the setting forth of these episodes I have narrated them as faithfully as the most conscientious realist could wish, and am therefore myself a true and faithful follower of the realistic school. I cannot be blamed because these things happen to me. If I sat down in my study to imagine the strange incidents to which I have in the past called attention, with no other object in view than to make my readers unwilling to retire for the night, to destroy the peace of mind of those who are good enough to purchase my literary wares, or to titillate till tense the nerve tissue of the timid who come to smile and who depart unstrung, then should I deserve the severest condemnation; but these things I do not do. I have a mission in life which I hold as sacred as my good friend Mr. Howells holds his. Such phases of life as I see I put down faithfully, and if the Fates in their wisdom have chosen to make of me the Balzac of the Supernatural, the Shakespeare of the Midnight Visitation, while elevating Mr. Howells to the high office of the Fielding of Massachusetts and its adjacent States, the Smollett of Boston, and the Sterne of Altruria, I can only regret that the powers have dealt more graciously with him than with me, and walk my little way as gracefully as I know how. The slings and arrows of outrageous fortune I am prepared to suffer in all meekness of spirit; I accept them because it seems to me to be nobler in the mind so to do rather than by opposing to end them. And so to my story. I have prefaced it at such length for but one reason, and that is that I am aware that there will be those who will doubt the veracity of my tale, and I am anxious at the outset to impress upon all the unquestioned fact that what I am about to tell is the plain, unvarnished truth, and, as I have already said, it happened last Christmas Eve.

I regret to have to say so, for it sounds so much like the description given to other Christmas Eves by writers with a less conscientious regard for the truth than I possess, but the facts must be told, and I must therefore state that it was a wild and stormy night. The winds howled and moaned and made all sorts of curious noises, soughing through the bare limbs of the trees, whistling through the chimneys, and, with reckless disregard of my children's need of rest, slamming doors until my house seemed to be the centre of a bombardment of no mean order. It is also necessary to state that the snow, which had been falling all day, had clothed the lawns and house-tops in a dazzling drapery of white, and, not content with having done this to the satisfaction of all, was still falling, and, happily enough, as silently as usual. Were I the "wild romancer" that I have been called, I might have had the snow fall with a thunderous roar, but I cannot go to any such length. I love my fellow-beings, but there is a limit to my philanthropy, and I shall not have my snow fall noisily just to make a critic happy. I might do it to save his life, for I should hate to have a man die for the want of what I could give him with a stroke of my pen, and without any special effort, but until that emergency arises I shall not yield a jot in the manner of the falling of my snow.

Occasionally a belated home-comer would pass my house, the sleigh-bells strung about the ample proportions of his steed jingling loud above the roaring of the winds. My family had retired, and I sat alone in the glow of the blazing log—a very satisfactory gas affair—on the hearth. The flashing jet flames cast the usual grotesque shadows about the room, and my mind had thereby been reduced to that sensitive state which had hitherto betokened the coming of a visitor from other realms—a fact which I greatly regretted, for I was in no mood to be haunted. My first impulse, when I recognized the on-coming of that mental state which is evidenced by the goosing of one's flesh, if I may be allowed the expression, was to turn out the fire and go to bed. I have always found this the easiest method of ridding myself of unwelcome ghosts, and, conversely, I have observed that others who have been haunted unpleasantly have suffered in proportion to their failure to take what has always seemed to me to be the most natural course in the world—to hide their heads beneath the bed-covering. Brutus, when Caesar's ghost appeared beside his couch, before the battle of Philippi, sat up and stared upon the horrid apparition, and suffered correspondingly, when it would have been much easier and more natural to put his head under his pillow, and so shut out the unpleasant spectacle. That is the course I have invariably pursued, and it has never failed me. The most luminous ghost man ever saw is utterly powerless to shine through a comfortably stuffed pillow, or the usual Christmas-time quota of woollen blankets. But upon this occasion I preferred to await developments. The real truth is that I was about written out in the matter of visitations, and needed a reinforcement of my uncanny vein, which, far from being varicose, had become sclerotic, so dry had it been pumped by the demands to which it had been subjected by a clamorous, mystery-loving public. I had, I may as well confess it, run out of ghosts, and had come down to the writing of tales full of the horror of suggestion, leaving my readers unsatisfied through my failure to describe in detail just what kind of looking thing it was that had so aroused their apprehension; and one editor had gone so far as to reject my last ghost-story because I had worked him up to a fearful pitch of excitement, and left him there without any reasonable way out. I was face to face with a condition—which, briefly, was that hereafter that desirable market was closed to the products of my pen unless my contributions were accompanied by a diagram which should make my mysteries so plain that a little child could understand how it all came to pass. Hence it was that, instead of following my own convenience and taking refuge in my spectre-proof couch, I stayed where I was. I had not long to wait. The dial in my fuel-meter below-stairs had hardly had time to register the consumption of three thousand feet of gas before the faint sound of a bell reached my straining ears—which, by-the-way, is an expression I profoundly hate, but must introduce because the public demands it, and a ghost-story without straining ears having therefore no chance of acceptance by a discriminating editor. I started from my chair and listened intently, but the ringing had stopped, and I settled back to the delights of a nervous chill, when again the deathly silence of the night—the wind had quieted in time to allow me the use of this faithful, overworked phrase—was broken by the tintinnabulation of the bell. This time I recognized it as the electric bell operated by a push-button upon the right side of my front door. To rise and rush to the door was the work of a moment. It always is. In another instant I had flung it wide. This operation was singularly easy, considering that it was but a narrow door, and width was the last thing it could ever be suspected of, however forcible the fling. However, I did as I have said, and gazed out into the inky blackness of the night. As I had suspected, there was no one there, and I was at once convinced that the dreaded moment had come. I was certain that at the instant of my turning to re-enter my library I should see something which would make my brain throb madly and my pulses start. I did not therefore instantly turn, but let the wind blow the door to with a loud clatter, while I walked quickly into my dining-room and drained a glass of cooking-sherry to the dregs. I do not introduce the cooking-sherry here for the purpose of eliciting a laugh from the reader, but in order to be faithful to life as we live it. All our other sherry had been used by the queen of the kitchen for cooking purposes, and this was all we had left for the table. It is always so in real life, let critics say what they will.

This done, I returned to the library, and sustained my first shock. The unexpected had happened. There was still no one there. Surely this ghost was an original, and I began to be interested.

"Perhaps he is a modest ghost," I thought, "and is a little shy about manifesting his presence. That, indeed, would be original, seeing how bold the spectres of commerce usually are, intruding themselves always upon the privacy of those who are not at all minded to receive them."

Confident that something would happen, and speedily at that, I sat down to wait, lighting a cigar for company; for burning gas-logs are not as sociable as their hissing, spluttering originals, the genuine logs, in a state of ignition. Several times I started up nervously, feeling as if there was something standing behind me about to place a clammy hand upon my shoulder, and as many times did I resume my attitude of comfort, disappointed. Once I seemed to see a minute spirit floating in the air before me, but investigation showed that it was nothing more than the fanciful curling of the clouds of smoke I had blown from my lips. An hour passed and nothing occurred, save that my heart from throbbing took to leaping in a fashion which filled me with concern. A few minutes later, however, I heard a strange sound at the window, and my leaping heart stood still. The strain upon my tense nerves was becoming unbearable.

"At last!" I whispered to myself, hoarsely, drawing a deep breath, and pushing with all my force into the soft upholstered back of my chair. Then I leaned forward and watched the window, momentarily expecting to see it raised by unseen hands; but it never budged. Then I watched the glass anxiously, half hoping, half fearing to see something pass through it; but nothing came, and I began to get irritable.

I looked at my watch, and saw that it was half-past one o'clock.

"Hang you!" I cried, "whatever you are, why don't you appear, and be done with it? The idea of keeping a man up until this hour of the night!"

Then I listened for a reply; but there was none.

"What do you take me for?" I continued, querulously. "Do you suppose I have nothing else to do but to wait upon your majesty's pleasure? Surely, with all the time you've taken to make your début, you must be something of unusual horror."

Again there was no answer, and I decided that petulance was of no avail. Some other tack was necessary, and I decided to appeal to his sympathies—granting that ghosts have sympathies to appeal to, and I have met some who were so human in this respect that I have found it hard to believe that they were truly ghosts.

"I say, old chap," I said, as genially as I could, considering the situation—I was nervous, and the amount of gas consumed by the logs was beginning to bring up visions of bankruptcy before my eyes— "hurry up and begin your haunting—there's a good fellow. I'm a father—please remember that—and this is Christmas Eve. The children will be up in about three hours, and if you've ever been a parent yourself you know what that means. I must have some rest, so come along and show yourself, like the good spectre you are, and let me go to bed."

I think myself it was a very moving address, but it helped me not a jot. The thing must have had a heart of stone, for it never made answer.

"What?" said I, pretending to think it had spoken and I had not heard distinctly; but the visitant was not to be caught napping, even though I had good reason to believe that he had fallen asleep. He, she, or it, whatever it was, maintained a silence as deep as it was aggravating. I smoked furiously on to restrain my growing wrath. Then it occurred to me that the thing might have some pride, and I resolved to work on that.

"Of course I should like to write you up," I said, with a sly wink at myself. "I imagine you'd attract a good deal of attention in the literary world. Judging from the time it takes you to get ready, you ought to make a good magazine story—not one of those comic ghost-tales that can be dashed off in a minute, and ultimately get published in a book at the author's expense. You stir so little that, as things go by contraries, you'll make a stirring tale. You're long enough, I might say, for a three-volume novel—but—ah— I can't do you unless I see you. You must be seen to be appreciated. I can't imagine you, you know. Let's see, now, if I can guess what kind of a ghost you are. Um! You must be terrifying in the extreme— you'd make a man shiver in mid-August in mid-Africa. Your eyes are unfathomably green. Your smile would drive the sanest mad. Your hands are cold and clammy as a—ah—as a hot-water bag four hours after."

And so I went on for ten minutes, praising him up to the skies, and ending up with a pathetic appeal that he should manifest his presence. It may be that I puffed him up so that he burst, but, however that may be, he would not condescend to reply, and I grew angry in earnest.

"Very well," I said, savagely, jumping up from my chair and turning off the gas-log. "Don't! Nobody asked you to come in the first place, and nobody's going to complain if you sulk in your tent like Achilles. I don't want to see you. I could fake up a better ghost than you are anyhow—in fact, I fancy that's what's the matter with you. You know what a miserable specimen you are—couldn't frighten a mouse if you were ten times as horrible. You're ashamed to show yourself—and I don't blame you. I'd be that way too if I were you."

I walked half-way to the door, momentarily expecting to have him call me back; but he didn't. I had to give him a parting shot.

"You probably belong to a ghost union—don't you? That's your secret? Ordered out on strike, and won't do any haunting after sundown unless some other employer of unskilled ghosts pays his spooks skilled wages."

I had half a notion that the word "spook" would draw him out, for I have noticed that ghosts do not like to be called spooks any more than negroes like to be called "niggers." They consider it vulgar. He never yielded in his reserve, however, and after locking up I went to bed.

For a time I could not sleep, and I began to wonder if I had been just, after all. Possibly there was no spirit within miles of me. The symptoms were all there, but might not that have been due to my depressed condition—for it does depress a writer to have one of his best veins become sclerotic—I asked myself, and finally, as I went off to sleep, I concluded that I had been in the wrong all through, and had imagined there was something there when there really was not.

"Very likely the ringing of the bell was due to the wind," I said, as I dozed off. "Of course it would take a very heavy wind to blow the button in, but then—" and then I fell asleep, convinced that no ghost had ventured within a mile of me that night. But when morning came I was undeceived. Something must have visited us that Christmas Eve, and something very terrible; for while I was dressing for breakfast I heard my wife calling loudly from below.

"Henry!" she cried. "Please come down here at once."

"I can't. I'm only half shaved," I answered.

"Never mind that," she returned. "Come at once."

So, with the lather on one cheek and a cut on the other, I went below.

"What's the matter?" I asked.

"Look at that!" she said, pointing to my grandmother's hair-sofa, which stood in the hall just outside of my library door.

It had been black when we last saw it, but as I looked I saw that a great change had come over it.

It had turned white in a single night!

Now I can't account for this strange incident, nor can any one else, and I do not intend to try. It is too awful a mystery for me to attempt to penetrate, but the sofa is there in proof of all that I have said concerning it, and any one who desires can call and see it at any time. It is not necessary for them to see me; they need only ask to see the sofa, and it will be shown.

We have had it removed from the hall to the white-and-gold parlor, for we cannot bear to have it stand in any of the rooms we use.

THE MYSTERY OF BARNEY O'ROURKE

A very irritating thing has happened. My hired man, a certain Barney O'Rourke, an American citizen of much political influence, a good gardener, and, according to his lights, a gentleman, has got very much the best of me, and all because of certain effusions which from time to time have emanated from my pen. It is not often that one's literary chickens come home to roost in such a vengeful fashion as some of mine have recently done, and I have no doubt that as this story progresses he who reads will find much sympathy for me rising up in his breast. As the matter stands, I am torn with conflicting emotions. I am very fond of Barney, and I have always found him truthful hitherto, but exactly what to believe now I hardly know.

The main thing to bring my present trouble upon me, I am forced to believe, is the fact that my house has been in the past, and may possibly still be, haunted. Why my house should be haunted at all I do not know, for it has never been the scene of any tragedy that I am aware of. I built it myself, and it is paid for. So far as I am aware, nothing awful of a material nature has ever happened within its walls, and yet it appears to be, for the present at any rate, a sort of club-house for inconsiderate if not strictly horrid things, which is a most unfair dispensation of the fates, for I have not deserved it. If I were in any sense a Bluebeard, and spent my days cutting ladies' throats as a pastime; if I had a pleasing habit of inviting friends up from town over Sunday, and dropping them into oubliettes connecting my library with dark, dank, and snaky subterranean dungeons; if guests who dine at my house came with a feeling that the chances were, they would never return to their families alive—it might be different. I shouldn't and couldn't blame a house for being haunted if it were the dwelling-place of a bloodthirsty ruffian such as I have indicated, but that is just what it is not. It is not the home of a lover of fearful crimes. I would not walk ten feet for the pleasure of killing any man, no matter who he is. On the contrary, I would walk twenty feet to avoid doing it, if the emergency should ever arise, aye, even if it were that fiend who sits next me at the opera and hums the opera through from beginning to end. There have been times, I must confess, when I have wished I might have had the oubliettes to which I have referred constructed beneath my library and leading to the coal-bins or to some long-forgotten well, but that was two or three years ago, when I was in politics for a brief period, and delegations of willing and thirsty voters were daily and nightly swarming in through every one of the sixteen doors on the ground-floor of my house, which my architect, in a riotous moment, smuggled into the plans in the guise of "French windows." I shouldn't have minded then if the earth had opened up and swallowed my whole party, so long as I did not have to go with them, but under such provocation as I had I do not feel that my residence is justified in being haunted after its present fashion because such a notion entered my mind. We cannot help our thoughts, much less our notions, and punishment for that which we cannot help is not in strict accord with latter-day ideas of justice. It may occur to some hypercritical person to suggest that the English language has frequently been murdered in my den, and that it is its horrid corse which is playing havoc at my home, crying out to heaven and flaunting its bloody wounds in the face of my conscience, but I can pass such an aspersion as that by with contemptuous silence, for even if it were true it could not be set down as wilful assassination on my part, since no sane person who needs a language as much as I do would ever in cold blood kill any one of the many that lie about us. Furthermore, the English language is not dead. It may not be met with often in these days, but it is still encountered with sufficient frequency in the works of Henry James and Miss Libby to prove that it still lives; and I am told that one or two members of our consular service abroad can speak it—though as for this I cannot write with certainty, for I have never encountered one of these exceptions to the general rule.

The episode with which this narrative has to deal is interesting in some ways, though I doubt not some readers will prove sceptical as to its realism. There are suspicious minds in the world, and with these every man who writes of truth must reckon. To such I have only to say that it is my desire and intention to tell the truth as simply as it can be told by James, and as truthfully as Sylvanus Cobb ever wrote!

Now, then, the facts of my story are these:

In the latter part of last July, expecting a meeting of friends at my house in connection with a question of the good government of the city in which I honestly try to pay my taxes, I ordered one hundred cigars to be delivered at my residence. I ordered several other things at the same time, but they have nothing whatever to do with this story, because they were all—every single bottle of them— consumed at the meeting; but of the cigars, about which the strange facts of my story cluster, at the close of the meeting a goodly two dozen remained. This is surprising, considering that there were quite six of us present, but it is true. Twenty-four by actual count remained when the last guest left me. The next morning I and my family took our departure for a month's rest in the mountains. In the hurry of leaving home, and the worry of looking after three children and four times as many trunks, I neglected to include the cigars in my impedimenta, leaving them in the opened box upon my library table. It was careless of me, no doubt, but it was an important incident, as the sequel shows. The incidents of the stay in the hills were commonplace, but during my absence from home strange things were going on there, as I learned upon my return.

The place had been left in charge of Barney O'Rourke, who, upon my arrival, assured me that everything was all right, and I thanked and paid him.

"Wait a minute, Barney," I said, as he turned to leave me; "I've got a cigar for you." I may mention incidentally that in the past I had kept Barney on very good terms with his work by treating him in a friendly, sociable way, but, to my great surprise, upon this occasion he declined advances.

His face flushed very red as he observed that he had given up smoking.

"Well, wait a minute, anyhow," said I. "There are one or two things I want to speak to you about." And I went to the table to get a cigar for myself.

The box was empty!

Instantly the suspicion which has doubtless flashed through the mind of the reader flashed through my own—Barney had been tempted, and had fallen. I recalled his blush, and on the moment realized that in all my vast experience with hired men in the past I had never seen one blush before. The case was clear. My cigars had gone to help Barney through the hot summer.

"Well, I declare!" I cried, turning suddenly upon him. "I left a lot of cigars here when I went away, Barney."

"I know ye did, sorr," said Barney, who had now grown white and rigid. "I saw them meself, sorr. There was twinty-foor of 'em."

"You counted them, eh?" I asked, with an elevation of my eyebrows which to those who know me conveys the idea of suspicion.

"I did, sorr. In your absence I was responsible for everyt'ing here, and the mornin' ye wint awaa I took a quick invintery, sorr, of the removables," he answered, fingering his cap nervously. "That's how it was, sorr, and thim twenty-foor segyars was lyin' there in the box forninst me eyes."

"And how do you account for the removal of these removables, as you call them, Barney?" I asked, looking coldly at him. He saw he was under suspicion, and he winced, but pulled himself together in an instant.

"I expected the question, sorr," he said, calmly, "and I have me answer ready. Thim segyars was shmoked, sorr."

"Doubtless," said I, with an ill-suppressed sneer. "And by whom? Cats?" I added, with a contemptuous shrug of my shoulders.

His answer overpowered me, it was so simple, direct, and unexpected.

"Shpooks," he replied, laconically.

I gasped in astonishment, and sat down. My knees simply collapsed under me, and I could no more have continued to stand up than fly.

"What?" I cried, as soon as I had recovered sufficiently to gasp out the word.

"Shpooks," replied Barney. "Ut came about like this, sorr. It was the Froiday two wakes afther you left, I became un'asy loike along about nine o'clock in the avenin', and I fought I'd come around here and see if everything was sthraight. Me wife sez ut's foolish of me, sorr, and I sez maybe so, but I can't get ut out o' me head thot somet'ing's wrong.

"'Ye locked everything up safe whin ye left?' sez she.

"'I always does,' sez I.

"'Thin ut's a phwhim,' sez she.

"'No,' sez I. 'Ut's a sinsation. If ut was a phwim, ut'd be youse as would hov' it'; that's what I sez, severely loike, sorr, and out I shtarts. It was tin o'clock whin I got here. The noight was dark and blow-in' loike March, rainin' and t'underin' till ye couldn't hear yourself t'ink.

"I walked down the walk, sorr, an' barrin' the t'under everyt'ing was quiet. I troid the dures. All toight as a politician. Shtill, t'inks I, I'll go insoide. Quiet as a lamb ut was, sorr; but on a suddent, as I was about to go back home again, I shmelt shmoke!"

"Fire?" I cried, excitedly.

"I said shmoke, sorr," said Barney, whose calmness was now beautiful to look upon, he was so serenely confident of his position.

"Doesn't smoke involve a fire?" I demanded.

"Sometimes," said Barney. "It ought ye meant a conflagrashun, sorr. The shmoke I shmelt was segyars."

"Ah," I observed. "I am glad you are coming to the point. Go on. There *is* a difference."

"There is thot," said Barney, pleasantly, he was getting along so swimmingly. "This shmoke, as I say, was segyar shmoke, so I gropes me way cautious loike up the back sthairs and listens by the library dure. All quiet as a lamb. Thin, bold loike, I shteps into the room, and nearly drops wid the shcare I have on me in a minute. The room was dark as a b'aver hat, sorr, but in different shpots ranged round in the chairs was six little red balls of foire!"

"Barney!" I cried.

"Thrue, sorr," said he. "And tobacky shmoke rollin' out till you'd 'a' t'ought there was a foire in a segyar-store! Ut queered me, sorr, for a minute, and me impulse is to run; but I gets me courage up, springs across the room, touches the electhric button, an' bzt! every gas-jet on the flure loights up!"

"That was rash, Barney," I put in, sarcastically.

"It was in your intherest, sorr," said he, impressively.

"And you saw what?" I queried, growing very impatient.

"What I hope niver to see again, sorr," said Barney, compressing his lips solemnly. "*Six impty chairs,* sorr, wid six segyars as hoigh up from the flure as a man' s mout' , puffin' and a-blowin' out shmoke loike a chimbley! An' ivery oncet in a whoile the segyars would go down kind of an' be tapped loike as if wid a finger of a shmoker, and the ashes would fall off onto the flure!"

"Well?" said I. "Go on. What next?"

"I wanted to run awaa, sorr, but I shtood rutted to the shpot wid th' surproise I had on me, until foinally ivery segyar was burnt to a shtub and trun into the foireplace, where I found 'em the nixt mornin' when I came to clane up, provin' ut wasn't ony dhrame I'd been havin'."

I arose from my chair and paced the room for two or three minutes, wondering what I could say. Of course the man was lying, I thought. Then I pulled myself together.

"Barney," I said, severely, "what's the use? Do you expect me to believe any such cock-and-bull story as that?"

"No, sorr," said he. "But thim's the facts."

"Do you mean to say that this house of mine is haunted?" I cried.

"I don't know," said Barney, quietly. "I didn't t'ink so before."

"Before? Before what? When?" I asked.

"Whin you was writin' shtories about ut, sorr," said Barney, respectfully. "You've had a black horse-hair sofy turn white in a single noight, sorr, for the soight of horror ut's witnessed. You've had the hair of your own head shtand on ind loike tinpenny nails at what you've seen here in this very room, yourself, sorr. You've had ghosts doin' all sorts of t'ings in the shtories you've been writin' for years, and *you've always swore they was thrue, sorr.* I didn't believe 'em when I read 'em, but whin I see thim segyars bein' shmoked up before me eyes by invisible t'ings, I sez to meself, sez I, the boss ain't such a dommed loiar afther all. I've follyd your writin', sorr, very careful and close loike; an I don't see how, afther the tales you've told about your own experiences right here, you can say consistently that this wan o' mine ain't so!"

"But why, Barney," I asked, to confuse him, "when a thing like this happened, didn't you write and tell me?"

Barney chuckled as only one of his species can chuckle.

"Wroite an' tell ye?" he cried. "Be gorry, sorr, if I could wroite at all at all, ut's not you oi'd be wroitin' that tale to, but to the edithor of the paper that you wroite for. A tale loike that is wort' tin dollars to any man, eshpecially if ut's thrue. But I niver learned the art!"

And with that Barney left me overwhelmed. Subsequently I gave him the ten dollars which I think his story is worth, but I must confess that I am in a dilemma. After what I have said about my supernatural guests, I cannot discharge Barney for lying, but I'll be blest if I can quite believe that his story is accurate in every respect.

If there should happen to be among the readers of this tale any who have made a sufficiently close study of the habits of hired men and ghosts to be able to shed any light upon the situation, nothing would please me more than to hear from them.

I may add, in closing, that Barney has resumed smoking.

THE EXORCISM THAT FAILED

I — A JUBILEE EXPERIENCE

It has happened again. I have been haunted once more, and this time by the most obnoxious spook I have ever had the bliss of meeting. He is homely, squat, and excessively vulgar in his dress and manner. I have met cockneys in my day, and some of the most offensive varieties at that, but this spook absolutely outcocknifies them all, and the worst of it is I can't seem to rid myself of him. He has pursued me like an avenging angel for quite six months, and every plan of exorcism that I have tried so far has failed, including the receipt given me by my friend Peters, who, next to myself, knows more about ghosts that any man living. It was in London that I first encountered the vulgar little creature who has made my life a sore trial ever since, and with whom I am still coping to the best of my powers.

Starting out early in the morning of June 21, last summer, to witness the pageant of her Majesty Queen Victoria's Diamond Jubilee, I secured a good place on the corner of Northumberland Avenue and Trafalgar Square. There were two rows of people ahead of me, but I did not mind that. Those directly before me were short, and I could easily see over their heads, and, furthermore, I was protected from the police, who in London are the most dangerous people I have ever encountered, not having the genial ways of the Irish bobbies who keep the New York crowds smiling; who, when you are pushed into the line of march, merely punch you in a ticklish spot with the end of their clubs, instead of smashing your hair down into your larynx with their sticks, as do their London prototypes.

It was very comforting to me, having witnessed the pageant of 1887, when the Queen celebrated her fiftieth anniversary as a potentate, and thereby learned the English police system of dealing with crowds, to know that there were at least two rows of heads to be split open before my turn came, and I had formed the good resolution to depart as soon as the first row had been thus treated, whether I missed seeing the procession or not.

I had not been long at my post when the crowds concentrating on the line of march, coming up the avenue from the Embankment, began to shove intolerably from the rear, and it was as much as I could do to keep my place, particularly in view of the fact that the undersized cockney who stood in front of me appeared to offer no resistance to the pressure of my waistcoat against his narrow little back. It seemed strange that it should be so, but I appeared, despite his presence, to have nothing of a material nature ahead of me, and I found myself bent at an angle of seventy-five degrees, my feet firmly planted before me like those of a balky horse, restraining the onward tendency of the mob back of me.

Strong as I am, however, and stubborn, I am not a stone wall ten feet thick at the base, and the pressure brought to bear upon my poor self was soon too great for my strength, and I gradually encroached upon my unresisting friend. He turned and hurled a few remarks at me that are not printable, yet he was of no more assistance in withstanding the pressure than a marrowfat pea well cooked would have been.

"I'm sorry," I said, apologetically, "but I can't help it. If these policemen would run around to the rear and massacre some of the populace who are pushing me, I shouldn't have to shove you."

"Well, all I've got to say," he retorted, "is that if you don't keep your carcass out of my ribs I'll haunt you to your dying day."

"If you'd only put up a little backbone yourself you'd make it easier for me," I replied, quite hotly. "What are you, anyhow, a jellyfish or an India-rubber man?" He hadn't time to answer, for just as I spoke an irresistible shove from the crowd pushed me slap up against the man in the front row, and I was appalled to find the little fellow between us bulging out on both sides of me, crushed longitudinally from top to toe, so that he resembled a paper doll before the crease is removed from its middle, three-quarters open. "Great heavens!" I muttered. "What have I struck?"

"L-lul-let me out!" he gasped. "Don't you see you are squ-queezing my figure out of shape? Get bub-back, blank it!"

"I can't," I panted. "I'm sorry, but—"

"Sorry be hanged!" he roared. "This is my place, you idiot—"

This was too much for me, and in my inability to kick him with my foot I did it with my knee, and then, if I had not been excited, I should have learned the unhappy truth. My knee went straight through him and shoved the man ahead into the coat-tails of the bobbie in front. It was fortunate for me that it happened as it did, for the front-row man was wrathful enough to have struck me; but the police took care of him; and as he was carried away on a stretcher, the little jelly-fish came back into his normal proportions, like an inflated India-rubber toy.

"What the deuce are you, anyhow?" I cried, aghast at the spectacle.

"You'll find out before you are a year older!" he wrathfully answered. "I'll show you a shoving trick or two that you won't like, you blooming Yank!"

It made me excessively angry to be called a blooming Yank. I am a Yankee, and I have been known to bloom, but I can't stand having a low-class Britisher apply that term to me as if it were an opprobrious thing to be, so I tried once more to kick him with my knee. Again my knee passed through him, and this time took the policeman himself in the vicinity of his pistol-pocket. The irate officer turned quickly, raised his club, and struck viciously, not at the little creature, but at me. He didn't seem to see the jelly-fish. And then the horrid truth flashed across my mind. The thing in front of me was a ghost—a miserable relic of some bygone pageant, and visible only to myself, who have an eye to that sort of thing. Luckily the bobbie missed his stroke, and as I apologized, telling him I had St. Vitus's dance and could not control my unhappy leg, accompanying the apology with a half sovereign—both of which were accepted—peace reigned, and I shortly had the bliss of seeing the whole sovereign ride by—that is, I was told that the lady behind the parasol, which obscured everything but her elbow, was her Majesty the Queen.

Nothing more of interest happened between this and the end of the procession, although the little spook in front occasionally turned and paid me a compliment which would have cost any material creature his life. But that night something of importance did happen, and it has been going on ever since. The unlovely creature turned up in my lodgings just as I was about to retire, and talked in his rasping voice until long after four o'clock. I ordered him out, and he declined to go. I struck at him, but it was like hitting smoke.

"All right," said I, putting on my clothes. "If you won't get out, I will."

"That's exactly what I intended you to do," he said. "How do you like being shoved, eh? Yesterday was the 21st of June. I shall keep shoving you along, even as you shoved me, for exactly one year."

"Humph!" I retorted. "You called me a blooming Yank yesterday. I am. I shall soon be out of your reach in the great and glorious United States."

"Oh, as for that," he answered, calmly, "I can go to the United States. There are steamers in great plenty. I could even get myself blown across on a gale, if I wanted to—only gales are not always convenient. Some of 'em don't go all the way through, and connections are hard to make. A gale I was riding on once stopped in mid-ocean, and I had to wait a week before another came along, and it landed me in Africa instead of at New York."

"Got aboard the wrong gale, eh?" said I, with a laugh.

"Yes," he answered.

"Didn't you drown?" I cried, somewhat interested.

"Idiot!" he retorted. "Drown? How could I? You can't drown a ghost!"

"See here," said I, "if you call me an idiot again, I'll—I'll—"

"What?" he put in, with a grin. "Now just what will you do? You're clever, but *I'm a ghost!*"

"You wait and see!" said I, rushing angrily from the room. It was a very weak retort, and I frankly admit that I am ashamed of it, but it was the best I had at hand at the moment. My stock of repartee, like most men's vitality, is at its lowest ebb at four o'clock in the morning.

For three or four hours I wandered aimlessly about the city, and then returned to my room, and found it deserted; but in the course of my peregrinations I had acquired a most consuming appetite. Usually I eat very little breakfast, but this morning nothing short of a sixteen-course dinner could satisfy my ravening; so instead of eating my modest boiled egg, I sought the Savoy, and at nine o'clock entered the breakfast-room of that highly favored caravansary. Imagine my delight, upon entering, to see, sitting near one of the windows, my newly made acquaintances of the steamer, the Travises of Boston, Miss Travis looking more beautiful than ever and quite as haughty, by whom I was invited to join them. I accepted with alacrity, and was just about to partake of a particularly nice melon when who should walk in but that vulgar little spectre, hat jauntily placed on one side of his head, check-patterned trousers loud enough to wake the dead, and a green plaid vest about his middle that would be an indictable offence even on an American golf links.

"Thank Heaven they can't see the brute!" I muttered as he approached.

"Hullo, old chappie!" he cried, slapping me on my back. "Introduce me to your charming friends," and with this he gave a horrible low-born smirk at Miss Travis, to whom, to my infinite sorrow, by some accursed miracle, he appeared as plainly visible as he was to me.

"Really," said Mrs. Travis, turning coldly to me, "we—we can't, you know—we—Come, Eleanor. We will leave this *gentleman* with his *friend*, and have our breakfast sent to our rooms."

And with that they rose up and scornfully departed. The creature then sat down in Miss Travis's chair and began to devour her roll.

"See here," I cried, finally, "what the devil do you mean?"

"Shove number two," he replied, with his unholy smirk. "Very successful, eh? Werl, just you wait for number three. It will be what you Americans call a corker. By-bye."

And with that he vanished, just in time to spare me the humiliation of shying a pot of coffee at his head. Of course my appetite vanished with him, and my main duty now seemed to be to seek out the Travises and explain; so leaving the balance of my breakfast untasted, I sought the office, and sent my card up to Mrs. Travis. The response was immediate.

"The loidy says she's gone out, sir, and ain't likely to be back," remarked the top-lofty buttons, upon his return.

I was so maddened by this slight, and so thoroughly apprehensive of further trouble from the infernal shade, that I resolved without more ado to sneak out of England and back to America before the deadly blighting thing was aware of my intentions. I immediately left the Savoy, and sought the office of the Green Star Line, secured a room on the steamer sailing the next morning—the *Digestic*—from Liverpool, and was about packing up my belongings, when *it* turned up again.

"Going away, eh?"

"Yes," I replied, shortly, and then I endeavored to deceive him. "I've been invited down to Leamington to spend a week with my old friend Dr. Liverton."

"Oh, indeed!" he observed. "Thanks for the address. I will not neglect you during your stay there. Be prepared for a shove that will turn your hair gray. *Au revoir.*"

And he vanished, muttering the address I had given him—"Dr. Liverton, Leamington—Dr. Liverton." To which he added, "I won't forget *that*, not by a jugful."

I chuckled softly to myself as he disappeared. "He's clever, but— there are others," I said, delighted at the ease with which I had rid myself of him; and then eating a hearty luncheon, I took the train to Liverpool, where next morning I embarked on the *Digestic* for New York.

II—AN UNHAPPY VOYAGE

The sense of relief that swept over me when the great anchor of the *Digestic* came up from the unstrained quality of the Mersey, and I thought of the fact that shortly a vast ocean would roll between me and that fearful spook, was one of the most delightful emotions that it has ever been my good fortune to experience. Now all seemed serene, and I sought my cabin belowstairs, whistling gayly; but, alas! how fleeting is happiness, even to a whistler!

As I drew near to the room which I had fondly supposed was to be my own exclusively I heard profane remarks issuing therefrom. There was condemnation of the soap; there was perdition for the lighting apparatus; there were maledictions upon the location of the port, and the bedding was excommunicate.

"This is strange," said I to the steward. "I have engaged this room for the passage. I hear somebody in there."

"Not at all, sir," said he, opening the door; "it is empty." And to him it undoubtedly appeared to be so.

"But," I cried, "didn't you hear anything?"

"Yes, I did," he said, candidly; "but I supposed you was a ventriloquist, sir, and was a-puttin' up of a game on me."

Here the steward smiled, and I was too angry to retort. And then — Well, you have guessed it. *He* turned up — and more vulgar than ever.

"Hullo!" he said, nonchalantly, fooling with a suit-case. "Going over?"

"Oh no!" I replied, sarcastic. "Just out for a swim. When we get off the Banks I'm going to jump overboard and swim to the Azores on a wager."

"How much?" he asked.

"Five bob," said I, feeling that he could not grasp a larger amount.

"Humph!" he ejaculated. "I'd rather drive a cab — as I used to."

"Ah?" said I. "That's what you were, eh? A cab-driver. Takes a mighty mind to be that, eh? Splendid intellectual effort to drive a cab from the Reform Club to the Bank, eh?"

I had hoped to wither him.

"Oh, I don't know," he answered, suavely. "I'll tell you this, though: I'd rather go from the Club to the Bank on my hansom with me holding the reins than try to do it with Mr. Gladstone or the Prince o' Wiles on the box."

"Prince o' Wiles?" I said, with a withering manner.

"That's what I said," he retorted. "You would call him Prince of Whales, I suppose — like a Yank, a blooming Yank — because you think Britannia rules the waves."

I had to laugh; and then a plan of conciliation suggested itself. I would jolly him, as my political friends have it.

"Have a drink?" I asked.

"No, thanks; I don't indulge," he replied. "Let me offer you a cigar."

I accepted, and he extracted a very fair-looking weed from his box, which he handed me. I tried to bite off the end, succeeding only in biting my tongue, whereat the presence roared with laughter.

"What's the joke now?" I queried, irritated.

"You," he answered. "The idea of any one's being fool enough to try to bite off the end of a spook cigar strikes me as funny."

From that moment all thought of conciliation vanished, and I resorted to abuse.

"You are a low-born thing!" I shouted. "And if you don't get out of here right away I'll break every bone in your body."

"Very well," he answered, coolly, scribbling on a pad close at hand. "There's the address."

"What address?" I asked.

"Of the cemetery where those bones you are going to break are to be found. You go in by the side gate, and ask any of the grave-diggers where—"

"You infernal scoundrel!" I shrieked, "this is my room. I have bought and paid for it, and I intend to have it. Do you hear?"

His response was merely the clapping of his hands together, and in a stage-whisper, leaning towards me, he said:

"Bravo! Bravo! You are great. I think you could do Lear. Say those last words again, will you?"

His calmness was too much for me, and I lost all control of myself. Picking up the water-bottle, I hurled it at him with all the force at my command. It crashed through him and struck the mirror over the wash-stand, and as the shattered glass fell with a loud noise to the floor the door to my state-room opened, and the captain of the ship, flanked by the room steward and the doctor, stood at the opening.

"What's all this about?" said the captain, addressing me.

"I have engaged this room for myself alone," I said, trembling in my rage, "and I object to that person's presence." Here I pointed at the intruder.

"What person's presence?" demanded the captain, looking at the spot where the haunting thing sat grinning indecently.

"What person?" I roared, forgetting the situation for the moment. "Why, him—it—whatever you choose to call it. He's settled down here, and has been black-guarding me for twenty minutes, and, damn it, captain, I won't stand it!"

"It's a clear case," said the captain, with a sigh, turning and addressing the doctor. "Have you a strait-jacket?"

"Thank you, captain," said I, calming down. "It's what he ought to have, but it won't do any good. You see, he's not a material thing. He's buried in Kensal Green Cemetery, and so the strait-jacket won't help us."

Here the doctor stepped into the room and took me gently by the arm. "Take off your clothes," he said, "and lie down. You need quiet."

"I?" I demanded, not as yet realizing my position. "Not by a long shot. Fire *him* out. That's all I ask."

"Take off your clothes and get into that bed," repeated the doctor, peremptorily. Then he turned to the captain and asked him to detail two of his sailors to help him. "He's going to be troublesome," he added, in a whisper. "Mad as a hatter."

I hesitate, in fact decline, to go through the agony of what followed again by writing of it in detail. Suffice it to say that the doctor persisted in his order that I should undress and go to bed, and I, conscious of the righteousness of my position, fought this determination, until, with the assistance of the steward and the two able-bodied seamen detailed by the captain at the doctor's request, I was forcibly unclad and thrown into the lower berth and strapped down. My wrath knew no bounds, and I spoke my mind as plainly as I knew how. It is a terrible thing to be sane, healthy, fond of deck-walking, full of life, and withal unjustly strapped to a lower berth below the water-line on a hot day because of a little beast of a cockney ghost, and I fairly howled my sentiments.

On the second day from Liverpool two maiden ladies in the room next mine made representations to the captain which resulted in my removal to the steerage. They couldn't consent, they said, to listen to the shrieks of the maniac in the adjoining room.

And then, when I found myself lying on a cot in the steerage, still strapped down, who should appear but my little spectre.

"Well," he said, sitting on the edge of the cot, "what do you think of it now, eh? Ain't I a shover from Shoverville on the Push?"

"It's all right," I said, contemptuously. "But I'll tell you one thing, Mr. Spook: when I die and have a ghost of my own, that ghost will seek you out, and, by thunder, if it doesn't thrash the life out of you, I'll disown it!"

It seemed to me that he paled a bit at this, but I was too tired to gloat over a little thing like that, so I closed my eyes and went to sleep. A few days later I was so calm and rational that the doctor released me, and for the remainder of my voyage I was as free as any other person on board, except that I found myself constantly under surveillance, and was of course much irritated by the notion that my spacious stateroom was not only out of my reach, but probably in the undisputed possession of the cockney ghost.

After seven days of ocean travel New York was reached, and I was allowed to step ashore without molestation. But my infernal friend turned up on the pier, and added injury to insult by declaring in my behalf certain dutiable articles in my trunks, thereby costing me some dollars which I should much rather have saved. Still, after the incidents of the voyage, I thought it well to say nothing, and accepted the hardships of the experience in the hope that in the far distant future my spook would meet his and thrash the very death out of him.

Well, things went on. The cockney spook left me to my own devices until November, when I had occasion to lecture at a certain college in the Northwest. I travelled from my home to the distant platform, went upon it, was introduced by the proper functionary, and began my lecture. In the middle of the talk, who should appear in a vacant chair well down towards the stage but the cockney ghost, with a guffaw at a strong and not humorous point, which disconcerted me! I broke down and left the platform, and in the small room at the side encountered him.

"Shove the fourth!" he cried, and vanished.

It was then that I consulted Peters as to how best to be rid of him.

"There is no use of talking about it," I said to Peters, "the man is ruining me. Socially with the Travises I am an outcast, and I have no doubt they will tell about it, and my ostracism will extend. On the *Digestic* my sanity is seriously questioned, and now for the first time in my life, before some two thousand people, I break down in a public lecture which I have delivered dozens of times hitherto without a tremor. The thing cannot go on."

"I should say not," Peters answered. "Maybe I can help you to get rid of him, but I'm not positive about it; my new scheme isn't as yet perfected. Have you tried the fire-extinguisher treatment?"

I will say here, that Peters upon two occasions has completely annihilated unpleasant spectres by turning upon them the colorless and odorless liquids whose chemical action is such that fire cannot live in their presence.

"Fire, the vital spark, is the essential element of all these chaps," said he, "and if you can turn the nozzle of your extinguisher on that spook your ghost simply goes out."

"No, I haven't," I replied; "but I will the first chance I get." And I left him, hopeful if not confident of a successful exorcism.

On my return home I got out two of the extinguishers which were left in my back hall for use in case of an emergency, and tested one of them on the lawn. I merely wished to ascertain if it would work with spirit, and it did; it went off like a sodawater fountain loaded with dynamite, and I felt truly happy for the first time in many days.

"The vulgar little beast would better keep away from me now," I laughed. But my mirth was short-lived. Whether or not the obnoxious little chap had overheard, or from some hidden coign had watched my test of the fire-extinguisher I don't know, but when he came to my den that night he was amply protected against the annihilating effects of the liquid by a flaring plaid mackintosh, with a toque for his head, and the minute I started the thing squirting he turned his back and received the charge harmless on his shoulders. The only effect of the experiment was the drenching and consequent ruin of a pile of MSS. I had been at work on all day, which gave me another grudge against him. When the extinguisher had exhausted itself, the spectre turned about and fairly raised the ceiling with his guffaws, and when he saw my ruined pages upon the desk his mirth became convulsive.

"De-lightful!" he cried. "For an impromptu shove wherein I turn over the shoving to you in my own behalf, I never saw it equalled. Wouldn't be a bad thing if all writers would wet down their MSS. the same way, now would it?"

But I was too indignant to reply, and too chagrined over my failure to remain within-doors, so I rushed out and paced the fields for two hours. When I returned, he had gone.

III — THE SPIRIT TRIES TO MAKE REPARATION

Three weeks later he turned up once more. "Great Heavens!" I cried; "you back again?"

"Yes," he answered; "and I've come to tell you I'm mighty sorry about those ruined MSS. of yours. It is too bad that your whole day's work had to go for nothing."

"I think so myself," I retorted, coldly. "It's rather late in the day for you to be sorry, though. If you'll show your sincerity by going away and never crossing my path again, I may believe in you."

"Ah!" he said, "I've shown it in another way. Indeed I have. You know I have some conscience, though, to tell the truth, I haven't made much use of it. This time, however, as I considered the situation, a little voice rose up within me and said: 'It's all right, old chap, to be rough on this person; make him mad and shove him every which way; but don't destroy his work. His work is what he lives by—'"

"Yes," I interrupted, "and after what I told you on the steamer about what I would do to you when we got on even terms, you are not anxious to have me die. I know just how you feel. No thing likes to contemplate that paralysis that will surely fall upon you when my ghost begins to get in its fine work. I'm putting it in training now."

"You poor droll mortal!" laughed the cockney. "You poor droll mortal! As if I could ever be afraid of that! What is the matter with my going into training myself? Two can train, you know—even three. You almost make me feel sorry I tried to remedy the loss of those MSS."

Somehow or other a sense of some new misfortune came upon me.

"What?" I said, nervously.

"I say I'm almost sorry I tried to remedy the loss of those manuscripts. Composition, particularly poetry, is devilish hard for me—I admit it—and when I think of how I toiled over my substitutes for your ruined stuff, and see how very ungrateful you are, I grudge the effort."

"I don't understand you," I said, anxiously. "What do you mean?"

"I mean that I have written and sent out to the editors of the papers you write for a half a dozen poems and short stories."

"What has all that got to do with me?" I demanded.

"A great deal," he said. "You'll get the pay. *I signed your name to 'em.*"

"Y—you—you—you—did what?" I cried.

"Signed your name to 'em. There was a sonnet to 'A Coal Grab'— that was the longest of the lot. I think it will cover at least six magazine pages—"

"But," I cried, "a sonnet never contains more than fourteen lines— you—fool!"

"Oh yes, it does," he replied, calmly. "This one of yours had over four hundred. And then I wrote a three-page quatrain on 'Immortality,' which, if I do say it, is the funniest thing I ever read. I sent that to the *Weekly Methodist*."

"Good Lord, good Lord, good Lord!" I moaned. "A three-page quatrain!"

"Yes," he observed, calmly lighting one of his accursed cigars. "And you'll get all the credit."

A ray of hope entered my soul, and it enabled me to laugh hysterically. "They'll know it isn't mine," said I. "They know my handwriting at the office of the *Weekly Methodist*."

"No doubt," said he, dashing all my hopes to the ground. "But— ah— to remedy that drawback I took pains to find out what typewriter you used, and I had my quatrain copied on one of the same make."

"But the letter—the note with the manuscript?" I put in.

"Oh, I got over that very easily," he said. "I had that written also on the machine, on thin paper, and traced your signature at the bottom. It will be all right, my dear fellow. They'll never suspect."

And then, looking at the spirit-watch which he carried in his spectral fob-pocket, he vanished, leaving me immersed in the deepest misery of my life. Not content with ruining me socially, and as a lecturer; not satisfied with destroying me mentally on the seas, he had now attacked me on my most vulnerable point, my literary aspirations. I could not rest until I had read his "three-page quatrain" on "Immortality." Vulgar as I knew him to be, I felt confident that over my name something had gone out which even in my least self-respecting moods I could not tolerate. The only comfort that came to me was that his verses and his type-writing and his tracings of my autograph would be as spectral to others as to the eye not attuned to the seeing of ghosts. I was soon to be undeceived, however, for the next morning's mail brought to my home a dozen packages from my best "consumers," containing the maudlin frivolings of this—this—this—well, there is no polite word to describe him in any known tongue. I shall have to study the Aryan language—or Kipling—to find an epithet strong enough to apply to this especial case. Every point, every single detail, about these packages was convincing evidence of their contents having been of my own production. The return envelopes were marked at the upper corner with my name and address. The handwriting upon them was manifestly mine, although I never in my life penned those particular superscriptions. Within these envelopes were, I might say, pounds of MSS., apparently from my own typewriting machine, and signed in an autograph which would have deceived even myself.

And the stuff!

Stuff is not the word—in fact, there is no word in any language, however primitive and impolite, that will describe accurately the substance of those pages. And with each came a letter from the editor of the periodical to which the tale or poem had been sent *advising me to stop work for a while*, and one *suggested the Keeley cure!*

Immediately I sat down and wrote to the various editors to whom these productions had been submitted, explaining all—and every one of them came back to me unopened, with the average statement that until I had rested a year they really hadn't the time to read what I wrote; and my best friend among them, the editor of the *Weekly Methodist*, took the trouble to telegraph to my brother the recommendation that I should be looked after. And out of the mistaken kindness of his heart, he printed a personal in his next issue to the effect that his "valued contributor, Mr. Me, the public would regret to hear, was confined to his house by a sudden and severe attack of nervous prostration," following it up with an estimate of my career, which bore every mark of having been saved up to that time for use as an obituary.

And as I read the latter—the obituary—over, with tears in my eyes, what should I hear but the words, spoken at my back, clearly, but in unmistakable cockney accents,

"Shove the fifth!" followed by uproarious laughter. I grabbed up the ink-bottle and threw it with all my strength back of me, and succeeded only in destroying the wall-paper.

IV — THE FAILURE

The destruction of the wall-paper, not to mention the wiping out in a moment of my means of livelihood, made of the fifth shove an intolerable nuisance. Controlling myself with difficulty, I put on my hat and rushed to the telegraph office, whence I despatched a message, marked "Rush," to Peters.

"For Heaven's sake, complete your exorcism and bring it here at once," I wired him. "Answer collect."

Peters by no means soothed my agitation by his immediate and extremely flippant response.

"I don't know why you wish me to answer collect, but I suppose you do. So I answer as you request: Collect. What is it you are going to collect? Your scattered faculties?" he telegraphed. It was a mean sort of a telegram to send to a man in my unhappy state, and if he hadn't prepaid it I should never have forgiven him. I was mad enough when I received it, and a hot retort was about to go back, when the bothersome spook turned up and drew my mind off to other things.

"Well, what do you think of me?" he said, ensconcing himself calmly on my divan. "Pretty successful shover myself, eh?" Then he turned his eye to the inkspots on the wall. "Novel design in decoration, that. You ought to get employment in some wall-paper house. Given an accurate aim and plenty of ink, you can't be beaten for vigorous spatter-work."

I pretended to ignore his presence, and there was a short pause, after which he began again:

"Sulky, eh? Oh, well, I don't blame you. There's nothing in this world that can so harrow up one's soul as impotent wrath. I've heard of people bursting with it. I've had experiences in the art of irritation before this case. There was a fellow once hired my cab for an hour. Drove him all about London, and then he stopped in at a chop-house, leaving me outside. I waited and waited and waited, but he never came back. Left by the back door, you know. Clever trick, and for a while the laugh was on me; but when I got to the point where I could haunt him, I did it to the Regent's taste. I found him three years after my demise, and through the balance of his life pursued him everywhere with a phantom cab. If he went to church, I'd drive my spectre rig right down the middle aisle after him. If he called on a girl, there was the cab drawn up alongside of him in the parlor all the time, the horse stamping his foot and whinnying like all possessed. Of course no one else saw me or the horse or the cab, but he did—and, Lord! how mad he was, and how hopeless! Finally, in a sudden surge of wrath at his impotence, he burst, just like a soap-bubble. It was most amusing. Even the horse laughed."

"Thanks for the story," said I, wishing to anger him by my nonchalance. "I'll write it up."

"Do," he said. "It will make a clever sixth shove for me. People say your fancies are too wild and extravagant even now. A story like that will finish you at once."

"Again, thanks," said I, very calmly. "This time for the hint. Acting on your advice, I won't write it up."

"Don't," he retorted. "And be forever haunted with the idea. Either way, it suits me."

And he vanished once more.

The next morning Peters arrived at my house.

"I've come," he said, as he entered my den. "The scheme is perfected at last, and possibly you can use it. You need help of some kind. I can see that, just by reading your telegram. You're nervous as a cat. How do you heat your house?"

"What's that got to do with it?" I demanded, irritably. "You can't evaporate the little cuss."

"Don't want to," Peters replied. "That's been tried before, and it doesn't work. My scheme is a better one than that. Did you ever notice, while smoking in a house that is heated by a hot-air furnace, how, when a cloud of smoke gets caught in the current of air from the register, it is mauled and twisted until it gets free, or else is torn entirely apart?"

"Yes, I have," said I. "What of it?"

"Well, what's the matter with being genial with your old cockney until he gets in the habit of coming here every night, and bide your time until, without his knowing it, you can turn a blast from the furnace on him that will simply rend him to pieces?"

"By Jove!" I cried, delightedly. "You are a genius, old chap."

I rose and shook his hand until he remonstrated.

"Save your energy for him," said he. "You'll need it. It won't be a pleasant spectacle to witness when, in his struggles to get away, he is gradually dismembered. It will be something like the drawing and quartering punishment of olden times."

I shuddered as I thought of it, and for a moment was disposed to reject the plan, but my weakness left me as I thought of the ruin that stared me in the face.

"Oh, I don't know," I said, shaking my head. "It will have its pleasurable side, however fearsome it may prove as a sight. This house is just fitted for the operation, particularly on warm days. I have seen times when the blasts of hot air from my furnace have blown one of my poems off my table across the room."

"Great Scott!" cried Peters. "What a cyclone of an air-box you must have!"

Fortunately the winter season was on, and we were able to test the capacity of the furnace, with gratifying results. A soap-bubble was blown, and allowed to float downward until the current was reached, and the novel shapes it took, as it was blown about the room in its struggles to escape before it burst, were truly wonderful. I doubted not for an instant, from what I then saw, that the little cad of a spectre that was ruining my life would soon meet his Nemesis. So convinced was I of the ultimate success of the plan that I could hardly wait patiently for his coming. I became morbidly anxious for the horrid spectacle which I should witness as his body was torn apart and gradually annihilated by the relentless output of my furnace flues. To my great annoyance, it was two weeks before he turned up again, and I was beginning to fear that he had in some wise got wind of my intentions, and was turning my disappointment over his absence into the sixth of his series of "shoves." Finally, however, my anxiety was set at rest by his appearance on a night especially adapted to a successful issue of the conspiracy. It was blowing great guns from the west, and the blasts of air, intermittent in their force, that came up through the flues were such that under other circumstances they would have annoyed me tremendously. Almost everything in the line of the current that issued from the register and passed diagonally across the room to my fireplace, and so on up the chimney, was disturbed. The effect upon particles of paper and the fringes on my chairs was almost that of a pneumatic tube on substances placed within it, and on one or two occasions I was seriously apprehensive of the manner in which the flames on the hearth leaped upward into the sooty heights of my chimney flues.

But when, as happened shortly, I suddenly became conscious that my spectre cockney had materialized, all my fears for the safety of my house fled, and I surreptitiously turned off the heat, so that once he got within range of the register I could turn it on again, and his annihilation would be as instantaneous as what my newspaper friends call an electrocution. And that was precisely where I made my mistake, although I must confess that what ensued when I got the nauseating creature within range was most delightful.

"Didn't expect me back, eh?" he said, as he materialized in my library. "Missed me, I suppose, eh?"

"I've missed you like the deuce!" I replied, cordially, holding out my hand as if welcoming him back, whereat he frowned suspiciously. "Now that I'm reconciled to your system, and know that there is no possible escape for me, I don't seem to feel so badly. How have you been, and what have you been doing?"

"Bah!" he retorted. "What's up now? You know mighty well you don't like me any better than you ever did. What funny little game are you trying to work on me now, eh?"

"Really, 'Arry," I replied, "you wrong me—and, by-the-way, excuse me for calling you 'Arry. It is the most appropriate name I can think of at the moment."

"Call me what you blooming please," he answered. "But remember you can't soft-soap me into believing you like me. B-r-r-r-r!" he added, shivering. "It's beastly cold in here. What you been doing—storing ice?"

"Well—there's a fire burning over there in the fireplace," said I, anxious to get him before the open chimney-place; for, by a natural law, that was directly in the line of the current.

He looked at me suspiciously, and then at the fireplace with equal mistrust; then he shrugged his shoulders with a mocking laugh that jarred.

"Humph!" he said. "What's your scheme? Got some patent explosive logs, full of chemicals, to destroy me?"

I laughed. "How suspicious you are!" I said.

"Yes—I always am of suspicious characters," he replied, planting himself immediately in front of the register, desirous no doubt of acting directly contrary to my suggestion.

My opportunity had come more easily than I expected.

"There isn't any heat here," said he.

"It's turned off. I'll turn it on for you," said I, scarcely able to contain myself with excitement—and I did.

Well, as I say, the spectacle was pleasing, but it did not work as I had intended. He was caught in the full current, not in any of the destroying eddyings of the side upon which I had counted to twist his legs off and wring his neck. Like the soap-bubble it is true, he was blown into various odd fantastic shapes, such as crullers resolve themselves into when not properly looked after, but there was no dismembering of his body. He struggled hard to free himself, and such grotesque attitudes as his figure assumed I never saw even in one of Aubrey Beardsley's finest pictures; and once, as his leg and right arm verged on the edge of one of the outside eddies, I hoped to see these members elongated like a piece of elastic until they snapped off; but, with a superhuman struggle, he got them free, with the loss only of one of his fingers, by which time the current had blown him across the room and directly in front of my fender. To keep from going up the chimney, he tried to brace himself against this with his feet, but missing the rail, as helpless as a feather, he floated, toes first, into the fireplace, and thence, kicking, struggling, and swearing profanely, disappeared into the flue.

It was too exciting a moment for me to laugh over my triumph, but shortly there came a nervous reaction which made me hysterical as I thought of his odd appearance; and then following close upon this came the dashing of my hopes.

An infernal misplaced, uncalled-for back gust, a diversion in which, thanks to an improper construction, my chimney frequently indulges, blew the unhappy creature back into the room again, strained, sprained, panting, minus the finger he had lost, and so angry that he quivered all over.

What his first words were I shall not repeat. They fairly seethed out of his turned and twisted soul, hissing like the escape-valve of an ocean steamer, and his eyes, as they fell upon mine, actually burned me.

"This settles it," he hissed, venomously. "I had intended letting you off with one more shove, but now, after your dastardly attempt to rend me apart with your damned hot-air furnace, I shall haunt you to your dying day; I shall haunt you so terribly that years before your final exit from this world you will pray for death. As a shover you have found me equal to everything, but since you prefer twisting, twisting be it. You shall hear from me again!"

He vanished, and, I must confess it, I threw myself upon my couch, weeping hot tears of despair.

Peters's scheme had failed, and I was in a far worse position than ever. Shoving I can stand, but the brief exhibition of twisting that I had had in watching his struggles with that awful cyclonic blast from below convinced me that there was something in life even more to be dreaded than the shoving he and I had been indulging in.

But there was a postscript, and now all is well again, because—but let us reserve the wherefore of the postscript for another, concluding chapter.

V — POSTSCRIPT

So hopeless was my estate now become that, dreading more than ever that which the inscrutable future held for me, I sat down and framed an advertisement, which I contemplated putting in all the newspapers, weeklies, and monthly periodicals, offering a handsome reward for any suggestion which might result in ridding me of the cockney ghost. The inventive mind of man has been able to cope successfully with rats and mice and other household pests. Why, then, should there not be somewhere in the world a person of sufficient ingenuity to cope with an obnoxious spirit? If rat-dynamite and rough on June-bugs were possible, why was it not likely that some as yet unknown person had turned his attention to spectrology, and evolved something in the nature of rough on ghosts, spectremelinite, or something else of an effective nature, I asked myself. It seemed reasonable to suppose that out of the millions of people in the world there were others than Peters and myself who had made a study of ghosts and methods of exorcising them, and if these persons could only be reached I might yet escape. Accordingly, I penned the advertisement about as follows:

> WANTED, by a young and rising author, who is pursued by a vindictive spirit,

A GHOST CURE.

> A liberal reward will be paid to any wizard, recognized or unrecognized, who will, before February I, 1898, send to me a detailed statement of a

GUARANTEED METHOD

of getting rid of

SPOOKS.

It is agreed that these communications shall be regarded as strictly confidential until such a time as through their medium the spirit is effectually

LAID,

after which time the cure will be exploited

FREE OF CHARGE

in the best advertising mediums of the day.

To this I appended an assumed name and a temporary address, and was about to send it out, when my friend Wilkins, a millionaire student of electricity, living in Florida, invited me to spend my Christmas holidays with him on Lake Worth.

"I've got a grand scheme," he wrote, "which I am going to test, and I'd like to have you present at the trial. Come down, if you can, and see my new electric sailboat and all-around dynamic Lone Fisherman."

The idea took hold of me at once. In my nervous state the change of scene would do me good. Besides, Wilkins was a delightful companion.

So, forgetting my woes for the moment, I packed my trunk and started South for Wilkins's Island. It was upon this trip that the vengeful spirit put in his first twist, for at Jacksonville I was awakened in the middle of the night by a person, whom I took to be the conductor, who told me to change cars. This I did, and falling asleep in the car to which I had changed, waked up the next morning to find myself speeding across the peninsula instead of going downward towards the Keys, as I should have done, landing eventually at a small place called Homosassa, on the Gulf coast.

Of course it was not the conductor of the first train who, under cover of the darkness, had led me astray, but the pursuing spirit, as I found out when, bewildered, I sat upon the platform of the station at Homosassa, wondering how the deuce I had got there. He turned up at that moment, and frankly gloated over the success of what he called shove the seventh, and twist the first.

"Nice place, this," said he, with a nauseating smirk. "So close to Lake Worth—eh? Only two days' ride on the choo-choo, if you make connections, and when changing take the right trains."

I pretended not to see him, and began to whistle the intermezzo from "Cavalleria Rusticana," to show how little I cared.

"Good plan, old chap," said he; "but it won't work. I know you are put out, in spite of the tunefulness of your soul. But wait for my second twist. You'll wish you'd struck a cyclone instead when that turn comes."

It was, as he suggested, at least two days before I was able to get to Wilkins at Lake Worth; but after I got there the sense of annoyance and the deep dejection into which I was plunged wore away, as well it might, for the test which I was invited to witness was most interesting. The dynamic Lone Fisherman was wonderful enough, but the electric sail-boat was a marvel. The former was very simple. It consisted of a reel operated by electricity, which, the moment a blue-fish struck the skid at the end of the line, reeled the fish in, and flopped it into a basket as easily and as surely as you please; but the principle of the sailboat was new.

"I don't need a breeze to sail anywhere," said Wilkins, as he hauled up the mainsail, which flapped idly in the still air. "For you see," he added, touching a button alongside of the tiller, "this button sets that big electric fan in the stern revolving, and the result is an artificial breeze which distends the sail, and there you are."

It was even as he said. A huge fan with a dozen flanges in the stern began to revolve with wonderful rapidity; in an instant the sails bellied out, and the *Horace J.*, as his boat was named, was speeding through the waters before the breeze thus created in record-breaking fashion.

"By Jove, Billie," I said, "this is a dandy!"

"Isn't it!" cried an old familiar voice at my elbow.

I turned as if stung. The spirit was with me again, prepared, I doubted not, for his second twist. I sprang from my seat, a sudden inspiration flashing upon me, jumped back of the revolving fan, and turning the full force of the wind it created upon my vindictive visitor, blew him fairly and squarely into the bulging sail.

"There, blast your cockney eyes!" I cried; "take that."

He tried to retort, but without avail. The wind that emanated from the fan fairly rammed his words back into his throat every time he opened his mouth to speak, and there he lay, flat against the canvas, fluttering like a leaf, powerless to escape.

"Hot air doesn't affect you much, you transparent jackass!" I roared. "Let me see how a stiff nor'easter suits your style of beauty."

I will not bore the reader with any further details of the Lake Worth experience. Suffice it to say that for five hours I kept the miserable thing a pneumatic prisoner in the concave surface of the sail. Try as he would, he could not escape, and finally, when Wilkins and I went ashore for the night, and the cockney ghost was released, he vanished, using unutterable language, and an idea came to me, putting which into operation, I at last secured immunity from his persecutions.

Returning to New York three days later, I leased a small office in a fire-proof power building not far from Madison Square, fitted it up as if for my own use, and had placed in the concealment of a closet at its easterly end the largest electric fan I could get. It was ten feet in diameter, and was provided with sixteen flanges. When it was in motion not a thing could withstand the blast that came from it. Tables, chairs, even a cut-glass inkstand weighing two pounds, were blown with a crash against the solid stone and iron construction back of the plaster of my walls. And then I awaited his coming.

Suffice it to say that he came, sat down calmly and unsuspecting in the chair I had had made for his especial benefit, and then the moment he began to revile me I turned on the power, the fan began to revolve, the devastating wind rushed down upon him with a roar, pinned him to the wall like a butterfly on a cork, and he was at last my prisoner—and he is my prisoner still. For three weeks has that wheel been revolving night and day, and despite all his cunning he cannot creep beyond its blustering influence, nor shall he ever creep therefrom while I have six hundred dollars per annum to pay for the rent and cost of power necessary to keep the fan going. Every once in a while I return and gloat over him; and I can tell by the movement of his lips that he is trying to curse me, but he cannot, for, even as Wilkins's fan blew his words of remonstrance back into his throat, so does my wheel, twice as powerful, keep his torrent of invective from greeting my ear.

I should be happy to prove the truth of all this by showing any curious-minded reader the spectacle which gives me so much joy, but I fear to do so lest the owners of the building, discovering the uses to which their office has been put, shall require me to vacate the premises.

Of course he may ultimately escape, through some failure of the machine to operate, but it is guaranteed to run five years without a break, so for that period at least I am safe, and by that time it may be that he will be satisfied to call things square. I shall be satisfied if he is.

Meanwhile, I devote my successful plan to the uses of all who may be troubled as I was, finding in their assumed gratitude a sufficient compensation for my ingenuity.

THURLOW'S CHRISTMAS STORY

I

(*Being the Statement of Henry Thurlow Author, to George Currier, Editor of the "Idler," a Weekly Journal of Human Interest.*)

I have always maintained, my dear Currier, that if a man wishes to be considered sane, and has any particular regard for his reputation as a truth-teller, he would better keep silent as to the singular experiences that enter into his life. I have had many such experiences myself; but I have rarely confided them in detail, or otherwise, to those about me, because I know that even the most trustful of my friends would regard them merely as the outcome of an imagination unrestrained by conscience, or of a gradually weakening mind subject to hallucinations. I know them to be true, but until Mr. Edison or some other modern wizard has invented a search-light strong enough to lay bare the secrets of the mind and conscience of man, I cannot prove to others that they are not pure fabrications, or at least the conjurings of a diseased fancy. For instance, no man would believe me if I were to state to him the plain and indisputable fact that one night last month, on my way up to bed shortly after midnight, having been neither smoking nor drinking, I saw confronting me upon the stairs, with the moonlight streaming through the windows back of me, lighting up its face, a figure in which I recognized my very self in every form and feature. I might describe the chill of terror that struck to the very marrow of my bones, and wellnigh forced me to stagger backward down the stairs, as I noticed in the face of this confronting figure every indication of all the bad qualities which I know myself to possess, of every evil instinct which by no easy effort I have repressed heretofore, and realized that that *thing* was, as far as I knew, entirely independent of my true self, in which I hope at least the moral has made an honest fight against the immoral always. I might describe this chill, I say, as vividly as I felt it at that moment, but it would be of no use to do so, because, however realistic it might prove as a bit of description, no man would believe that the incident really happened; and yet it did happen as truly as I write, and it has happened a dozen times since, and I am certain that it will happen many times again, though I would give all that I possess to be assured that never again should that disquieting creation of mind or matter, whichever it may be, cross my path. The experience has made me afraid almost to be alone, and I have found myself unconsciously and uneasily glancing at my face in mirrors, in the plate-glass of show-windows on the shopping streets of the city, fearful lest I should find some of those evil traits which I have struggled to keep under, and have kept under so far, cropping out there where all the world, all *my* world, can see and wonder at, having known me always as a man of right doing and right feeling. Many a time in the night the thought has come to me with prostrating force, what if that thing were to be seen and recognized by others, myself and yet not my whole self, my unworthy self unrestrained and yet recognizable as Henry Thurlow.

 I have also kept silent as to that strange condition of affairs which has tortured me in my sleep for the past year and a half; no one but myself has until this writing known that for that period of time I have had a continuous, logical dream-life; a life so vivid and so dreadfully real to me that I have found myself at times wondering which of the two lives I was living and which I was dreaming; a life in which that other wicked self has dominated, and forced me to a career of shame and horror; a life which, being taken up every time I sleep where it ceased with the awakening from a previous sleep, has made me fear to close my eyes in forgetfulness when others are near at hand, lest, sleeping, I shall let fall some speech that, striking on their ears, shall lead them to believe that in secret there is some wicked mystery connected with my life. It would be of no use for me to tell these things. It would merely serve to make my family and my friends uneasy about me if they were told in their awful detail, and so I have kept silent about them. To you alone, and now for the first time, have I hinted as to the troubles which have oppressed me for many days, and to you they are confided only because of the demand you have made that I explain to you the extraordinary complication in which the Christmas story sent you last week has involved me. You know that I am a man of dignity; that I am not a school-boy and a lover of childish tricks; and knowing that, your friendship, at least, should have restrained your tongue and pen when, through the former, on Wednesday, you accused me of perpetrating a trifling, and to you excessively embarrassing, practical joke—a charge which, at the moment, I was too overcome to refute; and through the latter, on Thursday, you reiterated the accusation, coupled with a demand for an explanation of my conduct satisfactory to yourself, or my immediate resignation from the staff of the *Idler*. To explain is difficult, for I am certain that you will find the explanation too improbable for credence, but explain I must. The alternative, that of resigning from your staff, affects not only my own welfare, but that of my children, who must be provided for; and if my post with you is taken from me, then are all resources gone. I have not the courage to face dismissal, for I have not sufficient confidence in my powers to please elsewhere to make me easy in my mind, or, if I could please elsewhere, the certainty of finding the immediate employment of my talents which is necessary to me, in view of the at present overcrowded condition of the literary field.

To explain, then, my seeming jest at your expense, hopeless as it appears to be, is my task; and to do so as completely as I can, let me go back to the very beginning.

In August you informed me that you would expect me to provide, as I have heretofore been in the habit of doing, a story for the Christmas issue of the *Idler*; that a certain position in the make-up was reserved for me, and that you had already taken steps to advertise the fact that the story would appear. I undertook the commission, and upon seven different occasions set about putting the narrative into shape. I found great difficulty, however, in doing so. For some reason or other I could not concentrate my mind upon the work. No sooner would I start in on one story than a better one, in my estimation, would suggest itself to me; and all the labor expended on the story already begun would be cast aside, and the new story set in motion. Ideas were plenty enough, but to put them properly upon paper seemed beyond my powers. One story, however, I did finish; but after it had come back to me from my typewriter I read it, and was filled with consternation to discover that it was nothing more nor less than a mass of jumbled sentences, conveying no idea to the mind—a story which had seemed to me in the writing to be coherent had returned to me as a mere bit of incoherence— formless, without ideas—a bit of raving. It was then that I went to you and told you, as you remember, that I was worn out, and needed a month of absolute rest, which you granted. I left my work wholly, and went into the wilderness, where I could be entirely free from everything suggesting labor, and where no summons back to town could reach me. I fished and hunted. I slept; and although, as I have already said, in my sleep I found myself leading a life that was not only not to my taste, but horrible to me in many particulars, I was able at the end of my vacation to come back to town greatly refreshed, and, as far as my feelings went, ready to undertake any amount of work. For two or three days after my return I was busy with other things. On the fourth day after my arrival you came to me, and said that the story must be finished at the very latest by October 15th, and I assured you that you should have it by that time. That night I set about it. I mapped it out, incident by incident, and before starting up to bed had actually written some twelve or fifteen hundred words of the opening chapter—it was to be told in four chapters. When I had gone thus far I experienced a slight return of one of my nervous chills, and, on consulting my watch, discovered that it was after midnight, which was a sufficient explanation of my nervousness: I was merely tired. I arranged my manuscripts on my table so that I might easily take up the work the following morning. I locked up the windows and doors, turned out the lights, and proceeded up-stairs to my room.

It was then that I first came face to face with myself—that other self, in which I recognized, developed to the full, every bit of my capacity for an evil life.

Conceive of the situation if you can. Imagine the horror of it, and then ask yourself if it was likely that when next morning came I could by any possibility bring myself to my work-table in fit condition to prepare for you anything at all worthy of publication in the *Idler*. I tried. I implore you to believe that I did not hold lightly the responsibilities of the commission you had intrusted to my hands. You must know that if any of your writers has a full appreciation of the difficulties which are strewn along the path of an editor, *I*, who have myself had an editorial experience, have it, and so would not, in the nature of things, do anything to add to your troubles. You cannot but believe that I have made an honest effort to fulfil my promise to you. But it was useless, and for a week after that visitation was it useless for me to attempt the work. At the end of the week I felt better, and again I started in, and the story developed satisfactorily until—*it* came again. That figure which was my own figure, that face which was the evil counterpart of my own countenance, again rose up before me, and once more was I plunged into hopelessness.

Thus matters went on until the 14th day of October, when I received your peremptory message that the story must be forthcoming the following day. Needless to tell you that it was not forthcoming; but what I must tell you, since you do not know it, is that on the evening of the 15th day of October a strange thing happened to me, and in the narration of that incident, which I almost despair of your believing, lies my explanation of the discovery of October 16th, which has placed my position with you in peril.

At half-past seven o'clock on the evening of October 15th I was sitting in my library trying to write. I was alone. My wife and children had gone away on a visit to Massachusetts for a week. I had just finished my cigar, and had taken my pen in hand, when my front -door bell rang. Our maid, who is usually prompt in answering summonses of this nature, apparently did not hear the bell, for she did not respond to its clanging. Again the bell rang, and still did it remain unanswered, until finally, at the third ringing, I went to the door myself. On opening it I saw standing before me a man of, I should say, fifty odd years of age, tall, slender, pale-faced, and clad in sombre black. He was entirely unknown to me. I had never seen him before, but he had about him such an air of pleasantness and wholesomeness that I instinctively felt glad to see him, without knowing why or whence he had come.

"Does Mr. Thurlow live here?" he asked.

You must excuse me for going into what may seem to you to be petty details, but by a perfectly circumstantial account of all that happened that evening alone can I hope to give a semblance of truth to my story, and that it must be truthful I realize as painfully as you do.

"I am Mr. Thurlow," I replied.

"Henry Thurlow, the author?" he said, with a surprised look upon his face.

"Yes," said I; and then, impelled by the strange appearance of surprise on the man's countenance, I added, "don't I look like an author?"

He laughed, and candidly admitted that I was not the kind of looking man he had expected to find from reading my books, and then he entered the house in response to my invitation that he do so. I ushered him into my library, and, after asking him to be seated, inquired as to his business with me.

His answer was gratifying at least He replied that he had been a reader of my writings for a number of years, and that for some time past he had had a great desire, not to say curiosity, to meet me and tell me how much he had enjoyed certain of my stories.

"I'm a great devourer of books, Mr. Thurlow," he said, "and I have taken the keenest delight in reading your verses and humorous sketches. I may go further, and say to you that you have helped me over many a hard place in my life by your work. At times when I have felt myself worn out with my business, or face to face with some knotty problem in my career, I have found much relief in picking up and reading your books at random. They have helped me to forget my weariness or my knotty problems for the time being; and to-day, finding myself in this town, I resolved to call upon you this evening and thank you for all that you have done for me."

Thereupon we became involved in a general discussion of literary men and their works, and I found that my visitor certainly did have a pretty thorough knowledge of what has been produced by the writers of to-day. I was quite won over to him by his simplicity, as well as attracted to him by his kindly opinion of my own efforts, and I did my best to entertain him, showing him a few of my little literary treasures in the way of autograph letters, photographs, and presentation copies of well-known books from the authors themselves. From this we drifted naturally and easily into a talk on the methods of work adopted by literary men. He asked me many questions as to my own methods; and when I had in a measure outlined to him the manner of life which I had adopted, telling him of my days at home, how little detail office-work I had, he seemed much interested with the picture—indeed, I painted the picture of my daily routine in almost too perfect colors, for, when I had finished, he observed quietly that I appeared to him to lead the ideal life, and added that he supposed I knew very little unhappiness.

The remark recalled to me the dreadful reality, that through some perversity of fate I was doomed to visitations of an uncanny order which were practically destroying my usefulness in my profession and my sole financial resource.

"Well," I replied, as my mind reverted to the unpleasant predicament in which I found myself, "I can't say that I know little unhappiness. As a matter of fact, I know a great deal of that undesirable thing. At the present moment I am very much embarrassed through my absolute inability to fulfil a contract into which I have entered, and which should have been filled this morning. I was due to-day with a Christmas story. The presses are waiting for it, and I am utterly unable to write it."

He appeared deeply concerned at the confession. I had hoped, indeed, that he might be sufficiently concerned to take his departure, that I might make one more effort to write the promised story. His solicitude, however, showed itself in another way. Instead of leaving me, he ventured the hope that he might aid me.

"What kind of a story is it to be?" he asked.

"Oh, the usual ghostly tale," I said, "with a dash of the Christmas flavor thrown in here and there to make it suitable to the season."

"Ah," he observed. "And you find your vein worked out?"

It was a direct and perhaps an impertinent question; but I thought it best to answer it, and to answer it as well without giving him any clew as to the real facts. I could not very well take an entire stranger into my confidence, and describe to him the extraordinary encounters I was having with an uncanny other self. He would not have believed the truth, hence I told him an untruth, and assented to his proposition.

"Yes," I replied, "the vein is worked out. I have written ghost stories for years now, serious and comic, and I am to-day at the end of my tether—compelled to move forward and yet held back."

"That accounts for it," he said, simply. "When I first saw you to-night at the door I could not believe that the author who had provided me with so much merriment could be so pale and worn and seemingly mirthless. Pardon me, Mr. Thurlow, for my lack of consideration when I told you that you did not appear as I had expected to find you."

I smiled my forgiveness, and he continued:

"It may be," he said, with a show of hesitation—"it may be that I have come not altogether inopportunely. Perhaps I can help you."

I smiled again. "I should be most grateful if you could," I said.

"But you doubt my ability to do so?" he put in. "Oh—well—yes—of course you do; and why shouldn't you? Nevertheless, I have noticed this: At times when I have been baffled in my work a mere hint from another, from one who knew nothing of my work, has carried me on to a solution of my problem. I have read most of your writings, and I have thought over some of them many a time, and I have even had ideas for stories, which, in my own conceit, I have imagined were good enough for you, and I have wished that I possessed your facility with the pen that I might make of them myself what I thought you would make of them had they been ideas of your own."

The old gentleman's pallid face reddened as he said this, and while I was hopeless as to anything of value resulting from his ideas, I could not resist the temptation to hear what he had to say further, his manner was so deliciously simple, and his desire to aid me so manifest. He rattled on with suggestions for a half-hour. Some of them were good, but none were new. Some were irresistibly funny, and did me good because they made me laugh, and I hadn't laughed naturally for a period so long that it made me shudder to think of it, fearing lest I should forget how to be mirthful. Finally I grew tired of his persistence, and, with a very ill-concealed impatience, told him plainly that I could do nothing with his suggestions, thanking him, however, for the spirit of kindliness which had prompted him to offer them. He appeared somewhat hurt, but immediately desisted, and when nine o'clock came he rose up to go. As he walked to the door he seemed to be undergoing some mental struggle, to which, with a sudden resolve, he finally succumbed, for, after having picked up his hat and stick and donned his overcoat, he turned to me and said:

"Mr. Thurlow, I don't want to offend you. On the contrary, it is my dearest wish to assist you. You have helped me, as I have told you. Why may I not help you?"

"I assure you, sir—" I began, when he interrupted me.

"One moment, please," he said, putting his hand into the inside pocket of his black coat and extracting from it an envelope addressed to me. "Let me finish: it is the whim of one who has an affection for you. For ten years I have secretly been at work myself on a story. It is a short one, but it has seemed good to me. I had a double object in seeking you out to-night. I wanted not only to see you, but to read my story to you. No one knows that I have written it; I had intended it as a surprise to my—to my friends. I had hoped to have it published somewhere, and I had come here to seek your advice in the matter. It is a story which I have written and rewritten and rewritten time and time again in my leisure moments during the ten years past, as I have told you. It is not likely that I shall ever write another. I am proud of having done it, but I should be prouder yet if it—if it could in some way help you. I leave it with you, sir, to print or to destroy; and if you print it, to see it in type will be enough for me; to see your name signed to it will be a matter of pride to me. No one will ever be the wiser, for, as I say, no one knows I have written it, and I promise you that no one shall know of it if you decide to do as I not only suggest but ask you to do. No one would believe me after it has appeared as *yours*, even if I should forget my promise and claim it as my own. Take it. It is yours. You are entitled to it as a slight measure of repayment for the debt of gratitude I owe you."

He pressed the manuscript into my hands, and before I could reply had opened the door and disappeared into the darkness of the street. I rushed to the sidewalk and shouted out to him to return, but I might as well have saved my breath and spared the neighborhood, for there was no answer. Holding his story in my hand, I re-entered the house and walked back into my library, where, sitting and reflecting upon the curious interview, I realized for the first time that I was in entire ignorance as to my visitor's name and address.

I opened the envelope hoping to find them, but they were not there. The envelope contained merely a finely written manuscript of thirty odd pages, unsigned.

And then I read the story. When I began it was with a half-smile upon my lips, and with a feeling that I was wasting my time. The smile soon faded, however; after reading the first paragraph there was no question of wasted time. The story was a masterpiece. It is needless to say to you that I am not a man of enthusiasms. It is difficult to arouse that emotion in my breast, but upon this occasion I yielded to a force too great for me to resist. I have read the tales of Hoffmann and of Poe, the wondrous romances of De La Motte Fouque, the unfortunately little-known tales of the lamented Fitz-James O'Brien, the weird tales of writers of all tongues have been thoroughly sifted by me in the course of my reading, and I say to you now that in the whole of my life I never read one story, one paragraph, one line, that could approach in vivid delineation, in weirdness of conception, in anything, in any quality which goes to make up the truly great story, that story which came into my hands as I have told you. I read it once and was amazed. I read it a second time and was—tempted. It was mine. The writer himself had authorized me to treat it as if it were my own; had voluntarily sacrificed his own claim to its authorship that he might relieve me of my very pressing embarrassment. Not only this; he had almost intimated that in putting my name to his work I should be doing him a favor. Why not do so, then, I asked myself; and immediately my better self rejected the idea as impossible. How could I put out as my own another man's work and retain my self-respect? I resolved on another and better course—to send you the story in lieu of my own with a full statement of the circumstances under which it had come into my possession, when that demon rose up out of the floor at my side, this time more evil of aspect than before, more commanding in its manner. With a groan I shrank back into the cushions of my chair, and by passing my hands over my eyes tried to obliterate forever the offending sight; but it was useless. The uncanny thing approached me, and as truly as I write sat upon the edge of my couch, where for the first time it addressed me.

"Fool!" it said, "how can you hesitate? Here is your position: you have made a contract which must be filled; you are already behind, and in a hopeless mental state. Even granting that between this and to-morrow morning you could put together the necessary number of words to fill the space allotted to you, what kind of a thing do you think that story would make? It would be a mere raving like that other precious effort of August. The public, if by some odd chance it ever reached them, would think your mind was utterly gone; your reputation would go with that verdict. On the other hand, if you do not have the story ready by to-morrow, your hold on the *Idler* will be destroyed. They have their announcements printed, and your name and portrait appear among those of the prominent contributors. Do you suppose the editor and publisher will look leniently upon your failure?"

"Considering my past record, yes," I replied. "I have never yet broken a promise to them."

"Which is precisely the reason why they will be severe with you. You, who have been regarded as one of the few men who can do almost any kind of literary work at will—you, of whom it is said that your 'brains are on tap'—will they be lenient with *you*? Bah! Can' t you see that the very fact of your invariable readiness heretofore is going to make your present unreadiness a thing incomprehensible?"

"Then what shall I do?" I asked. "If I can't, I can't, that is all."

"You can. There is the story in your hands. Think what it will do for you. It is one of the immortal stories—"

"You have read it, then?" I asked.

"Haven't you?"

"Yes—but—"

"It is the same," it said, with a leer and a contemptuous shrug. "You and I are inseparable. Aren't you glad?" it added, with a laugh that grated on every fibre of my being. I was too overwhelmed to reply, and it resumed: "It is one of the immortal stories. We agree to that. Published over your name, your name will live. The stuff you write yourself will give you present glory; but when you have been dead ten years people won't remember your name even—unless I get control of you, and in that case there is a very pretty though hardly a literary record in store for you."

Again it laughed harshly, and I buried my face in the pillows of my couch, hoping to find relief there from this dreadful vision.

"Curious," it said. "What you call your decent self doesn't dare look me in the eye! What a mistake people make who say that the man who won't look you in the eye is not to be trusted! As if mere brazenness were a sign of honesty; really, the theory of decency is the most amusing thing in the world. But come, time is growing short. Take that story. The writer gave it to you. Begged you to use it as your own. It is yours. It will make your reputation, and save you with your publishers. How can you hesitate?"

"I shall not use it!" I cried, desperately.

"You must—consider your children. Suppose you lose your connection with these publishers of yours?"

"But it would be a crime."

"Not a bit of it. Whom do you rob? A man who voluntarily came to you, and gave you that of which you rob him. Think of it as it is—and act, only act quickly. It is now midnight."

The tempter rose up and walked to the other end of the room, whence, while he pretended to be looking over a few of my books and pictures, I was aware he was eyeing me closely, and gradually compelling me by sheer force of will to do a thing which I abhorred. And I—I struggled weakly against the temptation, but gradually, little by little, I yielded, and finally succumbed altogether. Springing to my feet, I rushed to the table, seized my pen, and signed my name to the story.

"There!" I said. "It is done. I have saved my position and made my reputation, and am now a thief!"

"As well as a fool," said the other, calmly. "You don't mean to say you are going to send that manuscript in as it is?"

"Good Lord!" I cried. "What under heaven have you been trying to make me do for the last half hour?"

"Act like a sane being," said the demon. "If you send that manuscript to Currier he'll know in a minute it isn't yours. He knows you haven't an amanuensis, and that handwriting isn't yours. Copy it."

"True!" I answered. "I haven't much of a mind for details to-night. I will do as you say."

I did so. I got out my pad and pen and ink, and for three hours diligently applied myself to the task of copying the story. When it was finished I went over it carefully, made a few minor corrections, signed it, put it in an envelope, addressed it to you, stamped it, and went out to the mail-box on the corner, where I dropped it into the slot, and returned home. When I had returned to my library my visitor was still there.

"Well," it said, "I wish you'd hurry and complete this affair. I am tired, and wish to go."

"You can't go too soon to please me," said I, gathering up the original manuscripts of the story and preparing to put them away in my desk.

"Probably not," it sneered. "I'll be glad to go too, but I can't go until that manuscript is destroyed. As long as it exists there is evidence of your having appropriated the work of another. Why, can't you see that? Burn it!"

"I can't see my way clear in crime!" I retorted. "It is not in my line."

Nevertheless, realizing the value of his advice, I thrust the pages one by one into the blazing log fire, and watched them as they flared and flamed and grew to ashes. As the last page disappeared in the embers the demon vanished. I was alone, and throwing myself down for a moment's reflection upon my couch, was soon lost in sleep.

It was noon when I again opened my eyes, and, ten minutes after I awakened, your telegraphic summons reached me.

"Come down at once," was what you said, and I went; and then came the terrible *dénouement*, and yet a *dénouement* which was pleasing to me since it relieved my conscience. You handed me the envelope containing the story.

"Did you send that?" was your question.

"I did—last night, or rather early this morning. I mailed it about three o'clock," I replied.

"I demand an explanation of your conduct," said you.

"Of what?" I asked.

"Look at your so-called story and see. If this is a practical joke, Thurlow, it's a damned poor one."

I opened the envelope and took from it the sheets I had sent you—twenty-four of them.

They were every one of them as blank as when they left the paper-mill!

You know the rest. You know that I tried to speak; that my utterance failed me; and that, finding myself unable at the time to control my emotions, I turned and rushed madly from the office, leaving the mystery unexplained. You know that you wrote demanding a satisfactory explanation of the situation or my resignation from your staff.

This, Currier, is my explanation. It is all I have. It is absolute truth. I beg you to believe it, for if you do not, then is my condition a hopeless one. You will ask me perhaps for a *résumé* of the story which I thought I had sent you.

It is my crowning misfortune that upon that point my mind is an absolute blank. I cannot remember it in form or in substance. I have racked my brains for some recollection of some small portion of it to help to make my explanation more credible, but, alas! it will not come back to me. If I were dishonest I might fake up a story to suit the purpose, but I am not dishonest. I came near to doing an unworthy act; I did do an unworthy thing, but by some mysterious provision of fate my conscience is cleared of that.

Be sympathetic Currier, or, if you cannot, be lenient with me this time. *Believe, believe, believe,* I implore you. Pray let me hear from you at once.

(Signed) HENRY THURLOW.

II

(*Being a Note from George Currier, Editor of the "Idler" to Henry Thurlow, Author.*)

Your explanation has come to hand. As an explanation it isn't worth the paper it is written on, but we are all agreed here that it is probably the best bit of fiction you ever wrote. It is accepted for the Christmas issue. Enclosed please find check for one hundred dollars.

Dawson suggests that you take another month up in the Adirondacks. You might put in your time writing up some account of that dream-life you are leading while you are there. It seems to me there are possibilities in the idea. The concern will pay all expenses. What do you say?

(Signed) Yours ever, G. C.

THE DAMPMERE MYSTERY

Dawson wished to be alone; he had a tremendous bit of writing to do, which could not be done in New York, where his friends were constantly interrupting him, and that is why he had taken the little cottage at Dampmere for the early spring months. The cottage just suited him. It was remote from the village of Dampmere, and the rental was suspiciously reasonable; he could have had a ninety-nine years' lease of it for nothing, had he chosen to ask for it, and would promise to keep the premises in repair; but he was not aware of that fact when he made his arrangements with the agent. Indeed, there was a great deal that Dawson was not aware of when he took the place. If there hadn't been he never would have thought of going there, and this story would not have been written.

It was late in March when, with his Chinese servant and his mastiff, he entered into possession and began the writing of the story he had in mind. It was to be the effort of his life. People reading it would forget Thackeray and everybody else, and would, furthermore, never wish to see another book. It was to be the literature of all time—past and present and future; in it all previous work was to be forgotten, all future work was to be rendered unnecessary.

For three weeks everything went smoothly enough, and the work upon the great story progressed to the author's satisfaction; but as Easter approached something queer seemed to develop in the Dampmere cottage. It was undefinable, intangible, invisible, but it was there. Dawson's hair would not stay down. When he rose up in the morning he would find every single hair on his head standing erect, and plaster it as he would with his brushes dipped in water, it could not be induced to lie down again. More inconvenient than this, his silken mustache was affected in the same way, so that instead of drooping in a soft fascinating curl over his lip, it also rose up like a row of bayonets and lay flat against either side of his nose; and with this singular hirsute affliction there came into Dawson's heart a feeling of apprehension over something, he knew not what, that speedily developed into an uncontrollable terror that pervaded his whole being, and more thoroughly destroyed his ability to work upon his immortal story than ten inconsiderate New York friends dropping in on him in his busy hours could possibly have done.

"What the dickens is the matter with me?" he said to himself, as for the sixteenth time he brushed his rebellious locks. "What has come over my hair? And what under the sun am I afraid of? The idea of a man of my size looking under the bed every night for — for something — burglar, spook, or what I don't know. Waking at midnight shivering with fear, walking in the broad light of day filled with terror; by Jove! I almost wish I was Chung Lee down in the kitchen, who goes about his business undisturbed."

Having said this, Dawson looked about him nervously. If he had expected a dagger to be plunged into his back by an unseen foe he could not have looked around more anxiously; and then he fled, actually fled in terror into the kitchen, where Chung Lee was preparing his dinner. Chung was only a Chinaman, but he was a living creature, and Dawson was afraid to be alone.

"Well, Chung," he said, as affably as he could, "this is a pleasant change from New York, eh?"

"Plutty good," replied Chung, with a vacant stare at the pantry door. "Me likes Noo Lork allee same. Dampeemere kind of flunny, Mister Dawson."

"Funny, Chung?" queried Dawson, observing for the first time that the Chinaman's queue stood up as straight as a garden stake, and almost scraped the ceiling as its owner moved about. "Funny?"

"Yeppee, flunny," returned Chung, with a shiver. "Me no likee. Me flightened."

"Oh, come!" said Dawson, with an affected lightness. "What are you afraid of?"

"Slumting," said Chung. "Do' know what. Go to bled; no sleepee; pigtail no stay down; heart go thump allee night."

"By Jove!" thought Dawson; "he's got it too!"

"Evlyting flunny here," resumed Chung.

"Jack he no likee too."

Jack was the mastiff.

"What's the matter with Jack?" queried Dawson. "You don't mean to say Jack's afraid?"

"Do' know if he 'flaid," said Chung, "He growl most time."

Clearly there was no comfort for Dawson here. To rid him of his fears it was evident that Chung could be of no assistance, and Chung's feeling that even Jack was affected by the uncanny something was by no means reassuring. Dawson went out into the yard and whistled for the dog, and in a moment the magnificent animal came bounding up. Dawson patted him on the back, but Jack, instead of rejoicing as was his wont over this token of his master's affection, gave a yelp of pain, which was quite in accord with Dawson's own feelings, for gentle though the pat was, his hand after it felt as though he had pressed it upon a bunch of needles.

"What's the matter, old fellow?" said Dawson, ruefully rubbing the palm of his hand. "Did I hurt you?"

The dog tried to wag his tail, but unavailingly, and Dawson was again filled with consternation to observe that even as Chung's queue stood high, even as his own hair would not lie down, so it was with Jack's soft furry skin. Every hair on it was erect, from the tip of the poor beast's nose to the end of his tail, and so stiff withal that when it was pressed from without it pricked the dog within.

"There seems to be some starch in the air of Dampmere," said Dawson, thoughtfully, as he turned and walked slowly into the house. "I wonder what the deuce it all means?"

And then he sought his desk and tried to write, but he soon found that he could not possibly concentrate his mind upon his work. He was continually oppressed by the feeling that he was not alone. At one moment it seemed as if there were a pair of eyes peering at him from the northeast corner of the room, but as soon as he turned his own anxious gaze in that direction the difficulty seemed to lie in the southwest corner.

"Bah!" he cried, starting up and stamping his foot angrily upon the floor. "The idea! I, Charles Dawson, a man of the world, scared by — by — well, by nothing. I don't believe in ghosts — and yet — at times I do believe that this house is haunted. My hair seems to feel the same way. It stands up like stubble in a wheat-field, and one might as well try to brush the one as the other. At this rate nothing'll get done. I'll go to town and see Dr. Bronson. There's something the matter with me."

So off Dawson went to town.

"I suppose Bronson will think I'm a fool, but I can prove all I say by my hair," he said, as he rang the doctor's bell. He was instantly admitted, and shortly after describing his symptoms he called the doctor's attention to his hair.

If he had pinned his faith to this, he showed that his faith was misplaced, for when the doctor came to examine it, Dawson's hair was lying down as softly as it ever had. The doctor looked at Dawson for a moment, and then, with a dry cough, he said:

"Dawson, I can conclude one of two things from what you tell me. Either Dampmere is haunted, which you and I as sane men can't believe in these days, or else you are playing a practical joke on me. Now I don't mind a practical joke at the club, my dear fellow, but here, in my office hours, I can't afford the time to like anything of the sort. I speak frankly with you, old fellow. I have to. I hate to do it, but, after all, you've brought it on yourself."

"Doctor," Dawson rejoined, "I believe I'm a sick man, else this thing wouldn't have happened. I solemnly assure you that I've come to you because I wanted a prescription, and because I believe myself badly off."

"You carry it off well, Dawson," said the doctor, severely, "but I'll prescribe. Go back to Dampmere right away, and when you've seen the ghost, telegraph me and I'll come down."

With this Bronson bowed Dawson out, and the latter, poor fellow, soon found himself on the street utterly disconsolate. He could not blame Bronson. He could understand how Bronson could come to believe that, with his hair as the only witness to his woes, and a witness that failed him at the crucial moment, Bronson should regard his visit as the outcome of some club wager, in many of which he had been involved previously.

"I guess his advice is good," said he, as he walked along. "I'll go back right away—but meanwhile I'll get Billie Perkins to come out and spend the night with me, and we'll try it on him. I'll ask him out for a few days."

Suffice it to say that Perkins accepted, and that night found the two eating supper together outwardly serene. Perkins was quite interested when Chung brought in the supper.

"Wears his queue Pompadour, I see," he said, as he glanced at Chung's extraordinary head-dress.

"Yes," said Dawson, shortly.

"You wear your hair that way yourself," he added, for he was pleased as well as astonished to note that Perkins's hair was manifesting an upward tendency.

"Nonsense," said Perkins. "It's flat as a comic paper."

"Look at yourself in the glass," said Dawson.

Perkins obeyed. There was no doubt about it. His hair was rising! He started back uneasily.

"Dawson," he cried, "what is it? I've felt queer ever since I entered your front door, and I assure you I've been wondering why you wore your mustache like a pirate all the evening."

"I can't account for it. I've got the creeps myself," said Dawson, and then he told Perkins all that I have told you.

"Let's—let's go back to New York," said Perkins.

"Can't," replied Dawson. "No train."

"Then," said Perkins, with a shiver, "let's go to bed."

The two men retired, Dawson to the room directly over the parlor, Perkins to the apartment back of it. For company they left the gas burning, and in a short time were fast asleep. An hour later Dawson awakened with a start. Two things oppressed him to the very core of his being. First, the gas was out; and second, Perkins had unmistakably groaned.

He leaped from his bed and hastened into the next room.

"Perkins," he cried, "are you ill?"

"Is that you, Dawson?" came a voice from the darkness.

"Yes. Did—did you put out the gas?"

"No."

"Are you ill?"

"No; but I'm deuced uncomfortable What's this mattress stuffed with— needles?"

"Needles? No. It's a hair mattress. Isn't it all right?"

"Not by a great deal. I feel as if I had been sleeping on a porcupine. Light up the gas and let's see what the trouble is."

Dawson did as he was told, wondering meanwhile why the gas had gone out. No one had turned it out, and yet the key was unmistakably turned; and, what was worse, on ripping open Perkins's mattress, a most disquieting state of affairs was disclosed.

Every single hair in it was standing on end!

A half-hour later four figures were to be seen wending their way northward through the darkness—two men, a huge mastiff, and a Chinaman. The group was made up of Dawson, his guest, his servant, and his dog. Dampmere was impossible; there was no train until morning, but not one of them was willing to remain a moment longer at Dampmere, and so they had to walk.

"What do you suppose it was?" asked Perkins, as they left the third mile behind them.

"I don't know," said Dawson; "but it must be something terrible. I don't mind a ghost that will make the hair of living beings stand on end, but a nameless invisible something that affects a mattress that way has a terrible potency that I have no desire to combat. It's a mystery, and, as a rule, I like mysteries, but the mystery of Dampmere I'd rather let alone."

"Don't say a word about the—ah—the mattress, Charlie," said Perkins, after awhile. "The fellows'll never believe it."

"No. I was thinking that very same thing," said Dawson.

And they were both true to Dawson's resolve, which is possibly why the mystery of Dampmere has never been solved.

If any of my readers can furnish a solution, I wish they would do so, for I am very much interested in the case, and I truly hate to leave a story of this kind in so unsatisfactory a condition.

A ghost story without any solution strikes me as being about as useful as a house without a roof.

CARLETON BARKER, FIRST AND SECOND

My first meeting with Carleton Barker was a singular one. A friend and I, in August, 18—, were doing the English Lake District on foot, when, on nearing the base of the famous Mount Skiddaw, we observed on the road, some distance ahead of us, limping along and apparently in great pain, the man whose subsequent career so sorely puzzled us. Noting his very evident distress, Parton and I quickened our pace and soon caught up with the stranger, who, as we reached his side, fell forward upon his face in a fainting condition—as well he might, for not only must he have suffered great agony from a sprained ankle, but inspection of his person disclosed a most extraordinary gash in his right arm, made apparently with a sharp knife, and which was bleeding most profusely. To stanch the flow of blood was our first care, and Parton, having recently been graduated in medicine, made short work of relieving the sufferer's pain from his ankle, bandaging it about and applying such soothing properties as he had in his knapsack—properties, by the way, with which, knowing the small perils to which pedestrians everywhere are liable, he was always provided.

Our patient soon recovered his senses and evinced no little gratitude for the service we had rendered him, insisting upon our accepting at his hands, merely, he said, as a souvenir of our good -Samaritanship, and as a token of his appreciation of the same, a small pocket-flask and an odd diamond-shaped stone pierced in the centre, which had hung from the end of his watch-chain, held in place by a minute gold ring. The flask became the property of Parton, and to me fell the stone, the exact hue of which I was never able to determine, since it was chameleonic in its properties. When it was placed in my hands by our "grateful patient" it was blood -red; when I looked upon it on the following morning it was of a livid, indescribable hue, yet lustrous as an opal. To-day it is colorless and dull, as though some animating quality that it had once possessed had forever passed from it.

"You seem to have met with an accident," said Parton, when the injured man had recovered sufficiently to speak.

"Yes," he said, wincing with pain, "I have. I set out for Saddleback this morning—I wished to visit the Scales Tarn and get a glimpse of those noonday stars that are said to make its waters lustrous, and—"

"And to catch the immortal fish?" I queried.

"No," he replied, with a laugh. "I should have been satisfied to see the stars—and I did see the stars, but not the ones I set out to see. I have always been more or less careless of my safety, walking with my head in the clouds and letting my feet look out for themselves. The result was that I slipped on a moss-covered stone and fell over a very picturesque bit of scenery on to some more stones that, unfortunately, were not moss-covered."

"But the cut in your arm?" said Parton, suspiciously. "That looks as if somebody else had given it to you."

The stranger's face flushed as red as could be considering the amount of blood he had lost, and a look of absolute devilishness that made my flesh creep came into his eyes. For a moment he did not speak, and then, covering the delay in his answer with a groan of anguish, he said:

"Oh, that! Yes—I—I did manage to cut myself rather badly and—"

"I don't see how you could, though," insisted Parton. "You couldn't reach that part of yourself with a knife, if you tried."

"That's just the reason why you should see for yourself that it was caused by my falling on my knife. I had it grasped in my right hand, intending to cut myself a stick, when I slipped. As I slipped it flew from my hand and I landed on it, fortunately on the edge and not on the point," he explained, his manner far from convincing, though the explanation seemed so simple that to doubt it were useless.

"Did you recover the knife?" asked Parton. "It must have been a mighty sharp one, and rather larger than most people carry about with them on excursions like yours."

"I am not on the witness-stand, sir," returned the other, somewhat petulantly, "and so I fail to see why you should question me so closely in regard to so simple a matter—as though you suspected me of some wrongdoing."

"My friend is a doctor," I explained; for while I was quite as much interested in the incident, its whys and wherefores, as was Parton, I had myself noticed that he was suspicious of his chance patient, and seemingly not so sympathetic as he would otherwise have been. "He regards you as a case."

"Not at all," returned Parton. "I am simply interested to know how you hurt yourself—that is all. I mean no offence, I am sure, and if anything I have said has hurt your feelings I apologize."

"Don't mention it, doctor," replied the other, with an uneasy smile, holding his left hand out towards Parton as he spoke. "I am in great pain, as you know, and perhaps I seem irritable. I'm not an amiable man at best; as for the knife, in my agony I never thought to look for it again, though I suppose if I had looked I should not have found it, since it doubtless fell into the underbrush out of sight. Let it rest there. It has not done me a friendly service to-day and I shall waste no tears over it."

With which effort at pleasantry he rose with some difficulty to his feet, and with the assistance of Parton and myself walked on and into Keswick, where we stopped for the night. The stranger registered directly ahead of Parton and myself, writing the words, "Carleton Barker, Calcutta," in the book, and immediately retired to his room, nor did we see him again that night. After supper we looked for him, but as he was nowhere to be seen, we concluded that he had gone to bed to seek the recuperation of rest. Parton and I lit our cigars and, though somewhat fatigued by our exertions, strolled quietly about the more or less somnolent burg in which we were, discussing the events of the day, and chiefly our new acquaintance.

"I don't half like that fellow," said Parton, with a dubious shake of the head. "If a dead body should turn up near or on Skiddaw to-morrow morning, I wouldn't like to wager that Mr. Carleton Barker hadn't put it there. He acted to me like a man who had something to conceal, and if I could have done it without seeming ungracious, I'd have flung his old flask as far into the fields as I could. I've half a mind to show my contempt for it now by filling it with some of that beastly claret they have at the *table d'hôte* here, and chucking the whole thing into the lake. It was an insult to offer those things to us."

"I think you are unjust, Parton," I said. "He certainly did look as if he had been in a maul with somebody. There was a nasty scratch on his face, and that cut on the arm was suspicious; but I can't see but that his explanation was clear enough. Your manner was too irritating. I think if I had met with an accident and was assisted by an utter stranger who, after placing me under obligations to him, acted towards me as though I were an unconvicted criminal, I'd be as mad as he was; and as for the insult of his offering, in my eyes that was the only way he could soothe his injured feelings. He was angry at your suspicions, and to be entirely your debtor for services didn't please him. His gift to me was made simply because he did not wish to pay you in substance and me in thanks."

"I don't go so far as to call him an unconvicted criminal, but I'll swear his record isn't clear as daylight, and I'm morally convinced that if men's deeds were written on their foreheads Carleton Barker, esquire, would wear his hat down over his eyes. I don't like him. I instinctively dislike him. Did you see the look in his eyes when I mentioned the knife?"

"I did," I replied. "And it made me shudder."

"It turned every drop of blood in my veins cold," said Parton. "It made me feel that if he had had that knife within reach he would have trampled it to powder, even if every stamp of his foot cut his flesh through to the bone. Malignant is the word to describe that glance, and I'd rather encounter a rattle-snake than see it again."

Parton spoke with such evident earnestness that I took refuge in silence. I could see just where a man of Parton's temperament—which was cold and eminently judicial even when his affections were concerned—could find that in Barker at which to cavil, but, for all that, I could not sympathize with the extreme view he took of his character. I have known many a man upon whose face nature has set the stamp of the villain much more deeply than it was impressed upon Barker's countenance, who has lived a life most irreproachable, whose every act has been one of unselfishness and for the good of mankind; and I have also seen outward appearing saints whose every instinct was base; and it seemed to me that the physiognomy of the unfortunate victim of the moss-covered rock and vindictive knife was just enough of a medium between that of the irredeemable sinner and the sterling saint to indicate that its owner was the average man in the matter of vices and virtues. In fact, the malignancy of his expression when the knife was mentioned was to me the sole point against him, and had I been in his position I do not think I should have acted very differently, though I must add that if I thought myself capable of freezing any person's blood with an expression of my eyes I should be strongly tempted to wear blue glasses when in company or before a mirror.

"I think I'll send my card up to him, Jack," I said to Parton, when we had returned to the hotel, "just to ask how he is. Wouldn't you?"

"No!" snapped Parton. "But then I'm not you. You can do as you please. Don't let me influence you against him—if he's to your taste."

"He isn't at all to my taste," I retorted. "I don't care for him particularly, but it seems to me courtesy requires that we show a little interest in his welfare."

"Be courteous, then, and show your interest," said Parton. "I don't care as long as I am not dragged into it."

I sent my card up by the boy, who, returning in a moment, said that the door was locked, adding that when he had knocked upon it there came no answer, from which he presumed that Mr. Barker had gone to sleep.

"He seemed all right when you took his supper to his room?" I queried.

"He said he wouldn't have any supper. Just wanted to be left alone," said the boy.

"Sulking over the knife still, I imagine," sneered Parton; and then he and I retired to our room and prepared for bed.

I do not suppose I had slept for more than an hour when I was awakened by Parton, who was pacing the floor like a caged tiger, his eyes all ablaze, and laboring under an intense nervous excitement.

"What's the matter, Jack?" I asked, sitting up in bed.

"That d—ned Barker has upset my nerves," he replied. "I can't get him out of my mind."

"Oh, pshaw!" I replied. "Don't be silly. Forget him."

"Silly?" he retorted, angrily. "Silly? Forget him? Hang it, I would forget him if he'd let me—but he won't."

"What has he got to do with it?"

"More than is decent," ejaculated Parton. "More than is decent. He has just been peering in through that window there, and he means no good."

"Why, you're mad," I remonstrated. "He couldn't peer in at the window—we are on the fourth floor, and there is no possible way in which he could reach the window, much less peer in at it."

"Nevertheless," insisted Parton, "Carleton Barker for ten minutes previous to your waking was peering in at me through that window there, and in his glance was that same malignant, hateful quality that so set me against him to-day—and another thing, Bob," added Parton, stopping his nervous walk for a moment and shaking his finger impressively at me—"another thing which I did not tell you before because I thought it would fill you with that same awful dread that has come to me since meeting Barker—the blood from that man's arm, the blood that stained his shirt-sleeve crimson, that besmeared his clothes, spurted out upon my cuff and coat-sleeve when I strove to stanch its flow!"

"Yes, I remember that," said I.

"And now look at my cuff and sleeve!" whispered Parton, his face grown white.

I looked.

There was no stain of any sort whatsoever upon either!

Certainly there must have been something wrong about Carleton Barker.

II

The mystery of Carleton Barker was by no means lessened when next morning it was found that his room not only was empty, but that, as far as one could judge from the aspect of things therein, it had not been occupied at all. Furthermore, our chance acquaintance had vanished, leaving no more trace of his whereabouts than if he had never existed.

"Good riddance," said Parton. "I am afraid he and I would have come to blows sooner or later, because the mere thought of him was beginning to inspire me with a desire to thrash him. I'm sure he deserves a trouncing, whoever he is."

I, too, was glad the fellow had passed out of our ken, but not for the reason advanced by Parton. Since the discovery of the stainless cuff, where marks of blood ought by nature to have been, I goose-fleshed at the mention of his name. There was something so inexpressibly uncanny about a creature having a fluid of that sort in his veins. In fact, so unpleasantly was I impressed by that episode that I was unwilling even to join in a search for the mysteriously missing Barker, and by common consent Parton and I dropped him entirely as a subject for conversation.

We spent the balance of our week at Keswick, using it as our head-quarters for little trips about the surrounding country, which is most charmingly adapted to the wants of those inclined to pedestrianism, and on Sunday evening began preparations for our departure, discarding our knickerbockers and resuming the habiliments of urban life, intending on Monday morning to run up to Edinburgh, there to while away a few days before starting for a short trip through the Trossachs.

While engaged in packing our portmanteaux there came a sharp knock at the door, and upon opening it I found upon the hall floor an envelope addressed to myself. There was no one anywhere in the hall, and, so quickly had I opened the door after the knock, that fact mystified me. It would hardly have been possible for any person, however nimble of foot, to have passed out of sight in the period which had elapsed between the summons and my response.

"What is it?" asked Parton, observing that I was slightly agitated.

"Nothing," I said, desirous of concealing from him the matter that bothered me, lest I should be laughed at for my pains. "Nothing, except a letter for me."

"Not by post, is it?" he queried; to which he added, "Can't be. There is no mail here to-day. Some friend?"

"I don't know," I said, trying, in a somewhat feminine fashion, to solve the authorship of the letter before opening it by staring at the superscription. "I don't recognize the handwriting at all."

I then opened the letter, and glancing hastily at the signature was filled with uneasiness to see who my correspondent was.

"It's from that fellow Barker," I said.

"Barker!" cried Parton. "What on earth has Barker been writing to you about?"

"He is in trouble," I replied, as I read the letter.

"Financial, I presume, and wants a lift?" suggested Parton.

"Worse than that," said I, "he is in prison in London."

"Wha-a-at?" ejaculated Parton. "In prison in London? What for?"

"On suspicion of having murdered an innkeeper in the South of England on Tuesday, August 16th."

"Well, I'm sorry to say that I believe he was guilty," returned Parton, without reflecting that the 16th day of August was the day upon which he and I had first encountered Barker.

"That's your prejudice, Jack," said I. "If you'll think a minute you'll know he was innocent. He was here on August 16th—last Tuesday. It was then that you and I saw him for the first time limping along the road and bleeding from a wound in the shoulder."

"Was Tuesday the 16th?" said Parton, counting the days backward on his fingers. "That's a fact. It was—but it's none of my affair anyhow. It is too blessed queer for me to mix myself up in it, and I say let him languish in jail. He deserved it for something, I am sure-"

"Well, I'm not so confoundedly heartless," I returned, pounding the table with my fist, indignant that Parton should allow his prejudices to run away with his sense of justice. "I'm going to London to do as he asks."

"What does he want you to do? Prove an alibi?"

"Precisely; and I'm going and you're going, and I shall see if the landlord here won't let me take one of his boys along to support our testimony—at my own expense if need be."

"You're right, old chap," returned Parton, after a moment of internal struggle. "I suppose we really ought to help the fellow out of his scrape; but I'm decidedly averse to getting mixed up in an affair of any kind with a man like Carleton Barker, much less in an affair with murder in it. Is he specific about the murder?"

"No. He refers me to the London papers of the 17th and 18th for details. He hadn't time to write more, because he comes up for examination on Tuesday morning, and as our presence is essential to his case he was necessarily hurried."

"It's deucedly hard luck for us," said Parton, ruefully. "It means no Scotland this trip."

"How about Barker's luck?" I asked. "He isn't fighting for a Scottish trip—he's fighting for his life."

And so it happened that on Monday morning, instead of starting for Edinburgh, we boarded the train for London at Car-lisle. We tried to get copies of the newspapers containing accounts of the crime that had been committed, but our efforts were unavailing, and it was not until we arrived in London and were visited by Barker's attorneys that we obtained any detailed information whatsoever of the murder; and when we did get it we were more than ever regretful to be mixed up in it, for it was an unusually brutal murder. Strange to say, the evidence against Barker was extraordinarily convincing, considering that at the time of the commission of the crime he was hundreds of miles from the scene. There was testimony from railway guards, neighbors of the murdered innkeeper, and others, that it was Barker and no one else who committed the crime. His identification was complete, and the wound in his shoulder was shown almost beyond the possibility of doubt to have been inflicted by the murdered man in self-defence.

"Our only hope," said the attorney, gravely, "is in proving an alibi. I do not know what to believe myself, the chain of evidence against my client is so complete; and yet he asserts his innocence, and has stated to me that you two gentlemen could assist in proving it. If you actually encountered Carleton Barker in the neighborhood of Keswick on the 16th of this month, the whole case against him falls to the ground. If not, I fear his outlook has the gallows at the small end of the perspective."

"We certainly did meet a Carleton Barker at Keswick on Tuesday, August 16th," returned Parton; "and he was wounded in the shoulder, and his appearance was what might have been expected of one who had been through just such a frightful murder as we understand this to have been; but this was explained to us as due to a fall over rocks in the vicinity of the Scales Tarn—which was plausible enough to satisfy my friend here."

"And not yourself?" queried the attorney.

"Well, I don't see what that has to do with it," returned Parton. "As to the locality there is no question. He was there. We saw him, and others saw him, and we have taken the trouble to come down here to state the fact, and have brought with us the call-boy from the hotel, who can support our testimony if it is not regarded as sufficient. I advise you, however, as attorney for Barker, not to inquire too deeply into that matter, because I am convinced that if he isn't guilty of this crime—as of course he is not—he hasn't the cleanest record in the world. He has bad written on every line of his face, and there were one or two things connected with our meeting with him that mightn't be to his taste to have mentioned in court."

"I don't need advice, thank you," said the attorney, dryly. "I wish simply to establish the fact of his presence at Keswick at the hour of 5 P.M. on Tuesday, August 16th. That was the hour at which the murder is supposed—in fact, is proved—to have been committed. At 5.30, according to witnesses, my client was seen in the neighborhood, faint with loss of blood from a knife-wound in the shoulder. Barker has the knife-wound, but he might have a dozen of them and be acquitted if he wasn't in Frewenton on the day in question."

"You may rely upon us to prove that," said I. "We will swear to it. We can produce tangible objects presented to us on that afternoon by Barker—"

"I can't produce mine," said Parton. "I threw it into the lake."

"Well, I can produce the stone he gave me," said I, "and I'll do it if you wish."

"That will be sufficient, I think," returned the attorney. "Barker spoke especially about that stone, for it was a half of an odd souvenir of the East, where he was born, and he fortunately has the other half. The two will fit together at the point where the break was made, and our case will be complete."

The attorney then left us. The following day we appeared at the preliminary examination, which proved to be the whole examination as well, since, despite the damning circumstantial evidence against Barker, evidence which shook my belief almost in the veracity of my own eyes, our plain statements, substantiated by the evidence of the call-boy and the two halves of the oriental pebble, one in my possession and the other in Barker's, brought about the discharge of the prisoner from custody; and the "Frewenton Atrocity" became one of many horrible murders, the mystery of which time alone, if anything, could unravel.

After Barker was released he came to me and thanked me most effusively for the service rendered him, and in many ways made himself agreeable during the balance of our stay in London. Parton, however, would have nothing to do with him, and to me most of his attentions were paid. He always had a singularly uneasy way about him, as though he were afraid of some impending trouble, and finally after a day spent with him slumming about London—and a more perfect slummer no one ever saw, for he was apparently familiar with every one of the worst and lowest resorts in all of London as well as on intimate terms with leaders in the criminal world—I put a few questions to him impertinently pertinent to himself. He was surprisingly frank in his answers. I was quite prepared for a more or less indignant refusal when I asked him to account for his intimacy with these dregs of civilization.

"It's a long story," he said, "but I'll tell it to you. Let us run in here and have a chop, and I'll give you some account of myself over a mug of ale."

We entered one of the numerous small eating-houses that make London a delight to the lover of the chop in the fulness of its glory. When we were seated and the luncheon ordered Barker began.

"I have led a very unhappy life. I was born in India thirty-nine years ago, and while my every act has been as open and as free of wrong as are those of an infant, I have constantly been beset by such untoward affairs as this in which you have rendered such inestimable service. At the age of five, in Calcutta, I was in peril of my liberty on the score of depravity, although I never committed any act that could in any sense be called depraved. The main cause of my trouble at that time was a small girl of ten whose sight was partially destroyed by the fiendish act of some one who, according to her statement, wantonly hurled a piece of broken glass into one of her eyes. The girl said it was I who did it, although at the time it was done, according to my mother's testimony, I was playing in her room and in her plain view. That alone would not have been a very serious matter for me, because the injured child might have been herself responsible for her injury, but in a childish spirit of fear, afraid to say so, and, not realizing the enormity of the charge, have laid it at the door of any one of her playmates she saw fit. She stuck to her story, however, and there were many who believed that she spoke the truth and that my mother, in an endeavor to keep me out of trouble, had stated what was not true."

"But you were innocent, of course?" I said.

"I am sorry you think it necessary to ask that," he replied, his pallid face flushing with a not unnatural indignation; "and I decline to answer it," he added. "I have made a practice of late, when I am in trouble or in any way under suspicion, to let others do my pleading and prove my innocence. But you didn't mean to be like your friend Parton, I know, and I cannot be angry with a man who has done so much for me as you have—so let it pass. I was saying that standing alone the accusation of that young girl would not have been serious in its effects in view of my mother's testimony, had not a seeming corroboration come three days later, when another child was reported to have been pushed over an embankment and maimed for life by no less a person than my poor innocent self. This time I was again, on my mother's testimony, at her side; but there were witnesses of the crime, and they every one of them swore to my guilt, and as a consequence we found it advisable to leave the home that had been ours since my birth, and to come to England. My father had contemplated returning to his own country for some time, and the reputation that I had managed unwittingly to build up for myself in Calcutta was of a sort that made it easier for him to make up his mind. He at first swore that he would ferret out the mystery in the matter, and would go through Calcutta with a drag-net if necessary to find the possible other boy who so resembled me that his outrageous acts were put upon my shoulders; but people had be-gun to make up their minds that there was not only something wrong about me, but that my mother knew it and had tried to get me out of my scrapes by lying—so there was nothing for us to do but leave."

"And you never solved the mystery?" I queried.

"Well, not exactly," returned Barker, gazing abstractedly before him. "Not exactly; but I have a theory, based upon the bitterest kind of experience, that I know what the trouble is."

"You have a double?" I asked.

"You are a good guesser," he replied; "and of all unhanged criminals he is the very worst."

There was a strange smile on his lips as Carleton Barker said this. His tone was almost that of one who was boasting—in fact, so strongly was I impressed with his appearance of conceit when he estimated the character of his double, that I felt bold enough to say:

"You seem to be a little proud of it, in spite of all."

Barker laughed.

"I can't help it, though he has kept me on tender-hooks for a lifetime," he said. "We all feel a certain amount of pride in the success of those to whom we are related, either by family ties or other shackles like those with which I am bound to my murderous *alter ego*. I knew an Englishman once who was so impressed with the notion that he resembled the great Napoleon that he conceived the most ardent hatred for his own country for having sent the illustrious Frenchman to St. Helena. The same influence—a very subtle one—I feel. Here is a man who has maimed and robbed and murdered for years, and has never yet been apprehended. In his chosen calling he has been successful, and though I have been put to my trumps many a time to save my neck from the retribution that should have been his, I can't help admiring the fellow, though I'd kill him if he stood before me!"

"And are you making any effort to find him?"

"I am, of course," said Barker; "that has been my life-work. I am fortunately possessed of means enough to live on, so that I can devote all my time to unravelling the mystery. It is for this reason that I have acquainted myself with the element of London with which, as you have noticed, I am very familiar. The life these criminals are leading is quite as revolting to me as it is to you, and the scenes you and I have witnessed together are no more unpleasant to you than they are to me; but what can I do? The man lives and must be run down. He is in England, I am certain. This latest diversion of his has convinced me of that."

"Well," said I, rising, "you certainly have my sympathy, Mr. Barker, and I hope your efforts will meet with success. I trust you will have the pleasure of seeing the other gentleman hanged."

"Thank you," he said, with a queer look in his eyes, which, as I thought it over afterwards, did not seem to be quite as appropriate to his expression of gratitude as it might have been.

III

When Barker and I parted that day it was for a longer period than either of us dreamed, for upon my arrival at my lodgings I found there a cable message from New York, calling me back to my labors. Three days later I sailed for home, and five years elapsed before I was so fortunate as to renew my acquaintance with foreign climes. Occasionally through these years Parton and I discussed Barker, and at no time did my companion show anything but an increased animosity towards our strange Keswick acquaintance. The mention of his name was sufficient to drive Parton from the height of exuberance to a state of abject depression.

"I shall not feel easy while that man lives," he said. "I think he is a minion of Satan. There is nothing earthly about him."

"Nonsense," said I. "Just because a man has a bad face is no reason for supposing him a villain or a supernatural creature."

"No," Parton answered; "but when a man's veins hold blood that saturates and leaves no stain, what are we to think?"

I confessed that this was a point beyond me, and, by mutual consent, we dropped the subject.

One night Parton came to my rooms white as a sheet, and so agitated that for a few minutes he could not speak. He dropped, shaking like a leaf, into my reading-chair and buried his face in his hands. His attitude was that of one frightened to the very core of his being. When I questioned him first he did not respond. He simply groaned. I resumed my reading for a few moments, and then looking up observed that Parton had recovered somewhat and was now gazing abstractedly into the fire.

"Well," I said, "feeling better?"

"Yes," he answered, slowly. "But it was a shock."

"What was?" I asked. "You've told me nothing as yet."

"I've seen Barker."

"No!" I cried. "Where?"

"In a back alley down-town, where I had to go on a hospital call. There was a row in a gambling-hell in Hester Street. Two men were cut and I had to go with the ambulance. Both men will probably die, and no one can find any trace of the murderer; but I know who he is. He was Carleton Barker and no one else. I passed him in the alley on the way in, and I saw him in the crowd when I came out."

"Was he alone in the alley?" I asked. Parton groaned again.

"That's the worst of it," said he. "He was not alone. He was with Carleton Barker."

"You speak in riddles," said I.

"I saw in riddles," said Parton; "for as truly as I sit here there were two of them, and they stood side by side as I passed through, alike as two peas, and crime written on the pallid face of each."

"Did Barker recognize you?"

"I think so, for as I passed he gasped—both of them gasped, and as I stopped to speak to the one I had first recognized he had vanished as completely as though he had never been, and as I turned to address the other he was shambling off into the darkness as fast as his legs could carry him."

I was stunned. Barker had been mysterious enough in London. In New York with his double, and again connected with an atrocity, he became even more so, and I began to feel somewhat towards him as had Parton from the first. The papers next morning were not very explicit on the subject of the Hester Street trouble, but they confirmed Parton's suspicions in his and my own mind as to whom the assassins were. The accounts published simply stated that the wounded men, one of whom had died in the night and the other of whom would doubtless not live through the day, had been set upon and stabbed by two unknown Englishmen who had charged them with cheating at cards; that the assailants had disappeared, and that the police had no clew as to their whereabouts.

Time passed and nothing further came to light concerning the Barkers, and gradually Parton and I came to forget them. The following summer I went abroad again, and then came the climax to the Barker episode, as we called it. I can best tell the story of that climax by printing here a letter written by myself to Parton. It was penned within an hour of the supreme moment, and while it evidences my own mental perturbation in its lack of coherence, it is none the less an absolutely truthful account of what happened. The letter is as follows:

"LONDON, July 18, 18—.

"My Dear Parton,—You once said to me that you could not breathe easily while this world held Carleton Barker living. You may now draw an easy breath, and many of them, for the Barker episode is over. Barker is dead, and I flatter myself that I am doing very well myself to live sanely after the experiences of this morning.

"About a week after my arrival in England a horrible tragedy was enacted in the Seven Dials district. A woman was the victim, and a devil in human form the perpetrator of the crime. The poor creature was literally hacked to pieces in a manner suggesting the hand of Jack the Ripper, but in this instance the murderer, unlike Jack, was caught red-handed, and turned out to be no less a person than Carleton Barker. He was tried and convicted, and sentenced to be hanged at twelve o'clock to-day.

"When I heard of Barker's trouble I went, as a matter of curiosity solely, to the trial, and discovered in the dock the man you and I had encountered at Keswick. That is to say, he resembled our friend in every possible respect. If he were not Barker he was the most perfect imitation of Barker conceivable. Not a feature of our Barker but was reproduced in this one, even to the name. But he failed to recognize me. He saw me, I know, because I felt his eyes upon me, but in trying to return his gaze I quailed utterly before him. I could not look him in the eye without a feeling of the most deadly horror, but I did see enough of him to note that he regarded me only as one of a thousand spectators who had flocked into the court-room during the progress of the trial. If it were our Barker who sat there his dissemblance was remarkable. So coldly did he look at me that I began to doubt if he really were the man we had met; but the events of this morning have changed my mind utterly on that point. He was the one we had met, and I am now convinced that his story to me of his double was purely fictitious, and that from beginning to end there has been but one Barker.

"The trial was a speedy one. There was nothing to be said in behalf of the prisoner, and within five days of his arraignment he was convicted and sentenced to the extreme penalty—that of hanging—and noon to-day was the hour appointed for the execution. I was to have gone to Richmond to-day by coach, but since Barker's trial I have been in a measure depressed. I have grown to dislike the man as thoroughly as did you, and yet I was very much affected by the thought that he was finally to meet death upon the scaffold. I could not bring myself to participate in any pleasures on the day of his execution, and in consequence I gave up my Richmond journey and remained all morning in my lodgings trying to read. It was a miserable effort. I could not concentrate my mind upon my book—no book could have held the slightest part of my attention at that time. My thoughts were all for Carleton Barker, and I doubt if, when the clock hands pointed to half after eleven, Barker himself was more apprehensive over what was to come than I. I found myself holding my watch in my hand, gazing at the dial and counting the seconds which must intervene before the last dreadful scene of a life of crime. I would rise from my chair and pace my room nervously for a few minutes; then I would throw myself into my chair again and stare at my watch. This went on nearly all the morning—in fact, until ten minutes before twelve, when there came a slight knock at my door. I put aside my nervousness as well as I could, and, walking to the door, opened it.

"I wonder that I have nerve to write of it, Parton, but there upon the threshold, clad in the deepest black, his face pallid as the head of death itself and his hands shaking like those of a palsied man, stood no less a person than Carleton Barker!

"I staggered back in amazement and he followed me, closing the door and locking it behind him.

"'What would you do?' I cried, regarding his act with alarm, for, candidly, I was almost abject with fear.

"'Nothing—to you!' he said. 'You have been as far as you could be my friend. The other, your companion of Keswick'—meaning you, of course—'was my enemy.'

"I was glad you were not with us, my dear Parton. I should have trembled for your safety.

"'How have you managed to escape?' I asked.

"'I have not escaped,' returned Barker. 'But I soon shall be free from my accursed double.'

"Here he gave an unearthly laugh and pointed to the clock.

"'Ha, ha!' he cried. 'Five minutes more—five minutes more and I shall be free.'

"'Then the man in the dock was not you?' I asked.

"'The man in the dock,' he answered, slowly, 'is even now mounting the gallows, whilst I stand here.'

"He trembled a little as he spoke, and lurched forward like a drunken man; but he soon recovered himself, grasping the back of my chair convulsively with his long white fingers.

"'In two minutes more,' he whispered, 'the rope will be adjusted about his neck; the black cap is even now being drawn over his cursed features, and—'

"Here he shrieked with laughter, and, rushing to the window, thrust his head out and literally sucked the air into his lungs, as a man with a parched throat would have drank water. Then he turned and, tottering back to my side, hoarsely demanded some brandy.

"It was fortunately at hand, and precisely as the big bells in Westminster began to sound the hour of noon, he caught up the goblet and held it aloft.

"'To him!' he cried.

"And then, Parton, standing before me in my lodgings, as truly as I write, he remained fixed and rigid until the twelfth stroke of the bells sounded, when he literally faded from my sight, and the goblet, falling to the floor, was shattered into countless atoms!"